George Mackay Brown

was born in Stromness in the Orkney Islands in 1921. He studied at Newbattle Abbey under Edwin Muir and read English at Edinburgh University. He has published many books including plays, poems, novels and collections of short stories. Edwin Muir described his work as possessing 'a strangeness and magic rare anywhere in literature today'.

George Mackay Brown has seldom left Orkney since he completed his academic studies, and the imagery and history of the islands have been the inspiration for all his work.

His most recent novel, *Beside the Ocean of Time*, also published by Flamingo, was shortlisted for the 1994 Booker Prize.

MODERN CLASSIC

GEORGE MACKAY BROWN

A Time to Keep

and other stories

Flamingo
An Imprint of HarperCollinsPublishers

Flamingo
An Imprint of HarperCollins*Publishers*
77–85 Fulham Palace Road,
Hammersmith, London W6 8JB

Published by Flamingo 1996
9 8 7 6 5 4 3 2 1

First published in Great Britain by
The Hogarth Press Ltd 1969

Author photograph by Gunnie Moberg

ISBN 0 00 654866 0

Set in Bell

Printed and bound in Great Britain by
Caledonian International Book Manufacturing Ltd, Glasgow

To Mhairi Brown
(1891–1967)

Acknowledgements

The author makes acknowledgement to the Editors of *Argosy*, *The Cornhill Magazine* and *The Glasgow Herald* in which some of these stories originally appeared, and to Macmillan & Co. Ltd., in whose anthology *Winter's Tales 14* the story *The Whaler's Return* is included.

Contents

CELIA   1

A TIME TO KEEP   38

A TREADING OF GRAPES   63

ICARUS   77

THE STORY TELLER   82

THE WIRELESS SET   100

THE FIVE OF SPADES   107

THE WHALER'S RETURN   115

THE BRIGHT SPADE   131

TARTAN   135

A CARRIER OF STONES   141

THE EYE OF THE HURRICANE   155

Celia

1

THE Norwegian whaler *Erika* tied up at the pier in the middle of Monday afternoon, and when the pubs opened at five o'clock all six of the crew went into the Hamnavoe Bar. Per Bjorling the skipper was with them, but about seven o'clock he bought a full bottle of vodka and left them drinking their whiskies and lagers and went outside. It was getting dark. He walked along the street till he came to an opening that descended step by step to a small pier with a house on it. From inside the house came the thwack of a hammer driving nails into leather. One room of the house had a lamp burning in the window but the other room next the sea was dark. Per Bjorling was about to knock at the door when it was opened from inside. He smiled and raised his sailor's cap and went in.

'What kind of a man is it this time?' shouted a voice from the lighted room. 'Is it that bloody foreigner? . . .' All the people in the neighbouring houses could hear what was being said. Maisie Ness came to the end of her pier and stood listening, her head cocked to one side.

The hammer smacked on leather, a rapid tattoo.

The seaward room remained dark; or rather, the window flushed a little as if a poker had suddenly woken flames from the coal.

'Yes,' yelled the shoemaker, 'a bloody drunken foreign sailor.'

Then silence returned to the piers and one by one the lights went on in all the houses round about.

The *Erika* and three other Norwegian whalers caught the morning tide on Tuesday and it was quiet again in the harbour. In the house on the small pier the shoe-repairing began early, the leisurely smack of the hammer on the moulded leather in between periods of quiet stitching. At ten o'clock Maisie Ness from the next close came with a pair of shoes to be soled. She walked straight in through the open door and turned into the room on the left next the street. The shoemaker sat on his stool, his mouth full of tacks. Maisie laid her shoes on the bench, soles upward.

'Celia isn't up yet, surely. I don't hear her,' she said.

'Celia's a good girl,' said the shoemaker.

'I don't believe you've had your breakfast,' cried Maisie Ness, 'and it's past ten o'clock. You need your food, or you'll be ill same as you were in the winter-time.'

'I'll get my breakfast,' said the shoemaker. 'Just leave the shoes on the bench. All they need is rubber soles and a protector or two in the right heel to keep it level. You're an impudent woman. Ignorant too. Could you read the deep books that Celia reads? I don't believe you can sign your name. I'll get my breakfast all right. Celia's a good girl. Just keep your tongue off her.'

Maisie Ness went up the steps of the pier shaking her head. She managed to look pleased and outraged at the same time.

'Celia,' the shoemaker called out, 'I'll make you a cup of tea. Just you lie in bed for an hour or two yet.'

3

It was early spring. Darkness was still long but the light was slowly encroaching and the days grew colder. The last of the snow still scarred the Orphir hills. One sensed a latent fertility; under the hard earth the seeds were awake and astir; their long journey to blossom and ripeness was beginning. But in Hamnavoe, the fishermen's town, the lamps still had to be lit early.

On Tuesday night every week Mr Spence the jeweller paid his visit. He would hesitate at the head of the close, look swiftly right and left along the street, then quickly descend the steps.

The shoemaker heard his precise footsteps on the flagstones outside and immediately took down from the shelf the draught-board and the set of draughtsmen. He had the pieces arranged on the board before Mr Spence was at the threshold.

'Come in, Mr Spence,' he shouted, 'come in. I heard your feet.'

And Mr Spence, without a single glance at the dark seaward window, went straight into the work-room on the left, bending his head under the lintel and smiling in the lamplight. 'Well, Thomas,' he said.

They always played for about an hour, best of three games. Mr Spence generally lost. Perhaps he was a poor player; perhaps he was nervous (he shuffled and blinked and cleared his throat a good deal); perhaps he genuinely liked to give the shoemaker the pleasure of winning; perhaps he was anxious to get this empty ritual over with. They played this night without speaking, the old man in his leather apron and the middle-aged bachelor in his smart serge tailor-made suit. The shoemaker won two games right away, inside half an hour, so that there was no need that night to play a decider.

'You put up a very poor show tonight,' said the shoemaker.

'I'm not in the same class as you, Thomas,' said Mr Spence.

He went over to his coat hanging on a peg and brought

a half-bottle of whisky out of the pocket. 'Perhaps, Thomas,' he said, 'you'd care for a drink.'

'You know fine,' said the shoemaker, 'I never drink that filthy trash. The poison!'

'Then,' said Mr Spence, 'perhaps I'll go and see if Miss Celia would care to have a little drink. A toddy, seeing it's a cold night.'

'No,' said the shoemaker anxiously, 'I don't think you should do that. Or if you do, only a very small drop.'

But Mr Spence was already tiptoeing along the lobby towards the dark room, carrying the half-bottle in his hand. He tapped on the door, and opened it gently. The girl was bending over the black range, stabbing the coal with a poker. At once the ribs were thronged with red and yellow flames, and the shadow of the girl leapt over him before she herself turned slowly to the voice in the doorway.

'My dear,'' said Mr Spence.

4

'How are you, Thomas?' said Dr Wilson on the Wednesday morning, sitting down on the bench among bits and scrapings of leather.

'I'm fine,' said the shoemaker.

'The chest all right?'

'I still get a bit of a wheeze when the wind's easterly,' said the shoemaker, 'but I'm not complaining.'

There was silence in the room for a half-minute.

'And Celia?' said Dr Wilson.

'Celia's fine,' said the shoemaker. 'I wish she would eat more and get more exercise. I'm a nuisance to her, I keep her tied to the house. But she keeps her health. She's fine.'

'I'm glad to hear it,' said Dr Wilson.

'Celia's a good girl,' said the shoemaker.

'I know she's a good girl,' said Dr Wilson. Then his

voice dropped a tone. 'Thomas,' he said, 'I don't want to worry you, but there are complaints in the town.'

'She's a good girl,' said the old man, 'a very good girl to me.'

'Complaints,' said Dr Wilson quietly, 'that this is a house of bad repute. I'm not saying it, for I know you're both good people, you and Celia. But the scandal-mongers are saying it along the street. You know the way it is. I've heard it twenty times this past week if I've heard it once. That all kinds of men come here, at all hours of the night, and there's drinking and carrying-on. I don't want to annoy you, Thomas, but I think it's right you should know what they're saying in the public, Maisie Ness and the other women. All this worry is not good for your lungs.'

'*I* don't drink,' said the shoemaker. 'How do I know who comes and goes in the night? That Maisie Ness should have her tongue cut out. Celia has a sweetheart, Ronald Leask of Clett, and she's applied to be a member of the Kirk. The minister's coming to see her Friday evening. She's a good girl.'

'Perhaps I could see Celia for a minute?' said Dr Wilson and got to his feet.

'No,' said the shoemaker, 'she's sleeping. She needs her rest. She's sleeping late. Celia is a very good girl to me. If it wasn't for Celia I know I'd have died in the winter time.'

'Good morning, Thomas,' said Dr Wilson. 'I'll be back next Wednesday. You have plenty of tablets to be getting on with. Tell Celia I'm asking for her. Send for me if you need me, any time.'

5

'Go away,' said the shoemaker to Mr William Snoddy the builder's clerk. 'Just you go away from this house and never come back, never so much as darken the door again. I know what you're after. I'm not a fool exactly.'

'I want you to make me a pair of light shoes for the summer,' said Mr Snoddy. 'That's all I want.'

'Is it?' said the shoemaker. 'Then you can go some other place, for I have no intention of doing the job for you.'

They were standing at the door of the house on the pier. It was Wednesday evening and the lamp was burning in the work-room but the room next the sea was in darkness.

'Last Saturday,' said Mr Snoddy, 'at the pier-head, you promised to make me a pair of light shoes for the summer.'

'I didn't know then,' said the shoemaker, 'what I know now. You and your fancy-women. Think shame of yourself. You have a wife and three bairns waiting for you in your house at the South End. And all you can do is run after other women here, there and everywhere. I'm making no shoes for whore-mastering expeditions. You can take that for sure and certain.'

'You've been listening,' said Mr Snoddy, 'to cruel groundless gossip.'

'And I believe the gossip,' said the shoemaker. 'I don't usually believe gossip but I believe this particular piece of gossip. You're an immoral man.'

'There's such a thing as a court of law,' said Mr Snoddy, 'and if ever I hear of these slanders being repeated again, I'll take steps to silence the slanderers.'

'You'll have your work cut out,' said the shoemaker, 'because you've been seen going to this house and that house when the men have been away at the fishing. I've seen you with my own two eyes. And if you want names I'll supply them to you with pleasure.'

'Let's go inside,' said Mr Snoddy in a suddenly pleasant

voice, 'and we'll talk about something else. We'll have a game of draughts.'

The shoemaker stretched out foot and arm and blocked the door.

'Stay where you are,' he said. 'Just bide where you are. What's that you've got in the inside pocket of your coat, eh?'

'It's my wallet,' said Mr Snoddy, touching the bulge at his chest.

'It's drink,' said the shoemaker, 'it's spirits. I'm not exactly so blind or so stupid that I can't recognize the shape of a half-bottle of whisky. I allow no drink into this house. Understand that.'

'Please, Thomas,' said Mr Snoddy. 'It's a cold night.'

'Forby being a whore-master,' said the shoemaker, 'you're a drunkard. Never a day passed that you aren't three or four times in the pub. Just look in the mirror when you get home and see how red your nose is getting. I'm sorry for your wife and children.'

'I mind my own business.' said Mr Snoddy.

'That's fine,' said the shoemaker. 'That's very good. Just mind your own business and don't come bothering this house. There's one thing I have to tell you before you go.'

'What's that?' said Mr Snoddy.

'Celia is not at home,' shouted the old man. He suddenly stepped back into the lobby and slammed the door shut. Mr Snoddy stood alone in the darkness, his mouth twitching. Then he turned and began to walk up the pier slowly.

From inside the house came the sound of steel protectors being hammered violently into shoes.

Mr Snoddy's foot was on the first step leading up to the street when a hand tugged at his sleeve. He turned round. It was Celia. She had a gray shawl over her head and her hair was tucked into it. Her face in the darkness was an oval oblique shadow.

'Celia,' said Mr Snoddy in a shaking voice.

'Where are you off to so soon, Billy boy?' said Celia. 'Won't you stop and speak for a minute to a poor lonely girl?'

Mr Snoddy put his hands round her shoulders. She pushed him away gently.

'Billy,' she said, 'If you have a little drink on you I could be doing with it.'

The loud hammering went on inside the house.

Mr Snoddy took the flask from his inside pocket. 'I think, dear,' he said, 'where we're standing we're a bit in the public eye. People passing in the street. Maybe if we move into that corner . . .'

Together they moved to the wall of the watchmaker's house, into a segment of deeper darkness.

'Dear Celia,' muttered Mr Snoddy.

'Just one little mouthful,' said Celia. 'I believe it's gin you've gone and bought.'

6

Ronald Leask closed the door of the tractor shed. The whole field on the south side of the hill was ploughed now, a good day's work. He looked round him, stretched his aching arms, and walked slowly a hundred yards down to the beach. The boat was secure. There had been south-westerly winds and high seas for two days, but during that afternoon the wind had veered further west and dropped. He thought he would be able to set his lobster-creels the next morning, Friday, under the Hoy crags. The *Celia* rocked gently at the pier like a furled sea bird.

Ronald went back towards his house. He filled a bucket with water from the rain barrel at the corner. He stripped off his soiled jersey and shirt and vest and washed quickly, shuddering and gasping as the cold water slapped into his shoulders and chest. He carried the pail inside and kicked off his boots and trousers and finished his washing. Then he dried himself at the dead hearth and put on his best clothes – the white shirt and tartan tie, the dark Sunday suit, the pigskin shoes. He combed his wet fair hair till it clung to both sides of his head like bronze wings. His face looked back at him from the square tarnished mirror on the mantelpiece, red and complacent and healthy. He put on his beret and pulled it a little to one side.

Ronald wheeled his bicycle out of the lobby on to the road, mounted, and cycled towards Hamnavoe.

He passed three cars and a county council lorry and a young couple out walking. It was too dark to see their faces. As he freewheeled down into the town there were lights here and there in the houses. It would be a dark night, with no moon.

Ronald Leask left his bicycle at the head of the shoemaker's close and walked down the steps to the house. The lamp was lit in the old man's window but Celia's room, as usual, was dark. He knocked at the outer door. The clob–clob–clobbering of hammer against leather stopped. 'Who's that?' cried the old man sharply.

'It's me, Ronald.'

'Ronald,' said the shoemaker. 'Come in, Ronald.' He appeared at the door. 'I'm glad to see thee, Ronald.' He took Ronald's arm and guided him into the workroom. 'Come in, boy, and sit down.'

'How are you keeping, Thomas?' said Ronald.

'I'm fine, Ronald,' said the shoemaker, and coughed.

'And Celia?' said Ronald.

'Celia's fine,' said the shoemaker. 'She's wanting to see thee, I know that. It's not much of a life for a girl, looking

9

after a poor old thing like me. She'll be glad of your company.'

'Last time I came, last Thursday, I didn't get much of a reception,' said Ronald.

'Celia wasn't well that day,' said the shoemaker. 'She likes thee more than anybody, I can assure thee for that.' He went over to the door and opened it and shouted across the lobby, 'Celia, Ronald's here.'

There was no answer from the other room.

'She's maybe sleeping,' said the shoemaker. 'Poor Celia, she works too hard, looking after me. What she needs is a long holiday. We'll go and see her.'

The old man crossed the lobby on tiptoe and opened the door of Celia's room gently. 'Celia,' he said, 'are you all right?'

'Yes,' said Celia's voice from inside.

'Ronald's here,' said the shoemaker.

'I know,' said Celia. 'I heard him.'

'Well,' said the shoemaker sharply, 'he wants to speak to you. And I'm taking him in now, whether you want it or not. And I'm coming in too for a minute.'

The two men went into the room. They could just make out the girl's outline against the banked-up glow of the fire. They groped towards chairs and sat down.

'Celia,' said the shoemaker, 'light your lamp.'

'No,' said Celia, 'I like it best this way, in the darkness. Besides, I have no money for paraffin. I don't get many shillings from you to keep the house going, and bread and coal and paraffin cost dear.'

'Speak to her, Ronald,' said the shoemaker.

'I can't be bothered to listen to him,' said Celia. 'I'm not well.'

'What ails you?' said the shoemaker.

'I don't know,' said Celia. 'I'm just not well.'

'Celia,' said Ronald earnestly, 'there's an understanding between us. You know it and I know it and the whole of Hamnavoe knows it. Why are you behaving this way to me?'

'That's true,' said the shoemaker. 'You're betrothed to one another.'

'Not this again,' said Celia, 'when I'm sick.' Then she said in a low voice, 'I need something to drink.'

'Drink!' said the old man angrily. 'That's all your mind runs on, drink. Just you listen to Ronald when he's speaking to you.'

'Celia,' said Ronald, 'it's a year come April since I buried my mother and the croft of Clett has stood there vacant ever since, except for me and the dog.'

'And a fine croft it is,' said the shoemaker. 'Good sandy soil and a tractor in the shed and a first-rate boat in the bay.'

'I'm not listening,' said Celia.

'It needs a woman about the place,' said Ronald. 'I can manage the farm work and the fishing. But inside the house things are going to wrack and ruin. That's the truth. Celia, you promised six months ago to come to Clett.'

'So that's all you want, is it?' said Celia. 'A house-keeper.'

'No,' said Ronald, 'I want you for my wife. I love you.'

'He does love you,' said the shoemaker. 'And he's a good man. And he has money put by. And he works well at the farming and the fishing. He's a fellow any girl would be proud to have for a man.'

'I'm not well tonight,' said Celia. 'I would be the better of a glass of brandy.'

'And what's more,' said the shoemaker, 'you love him, because you told me with your own lips not a fortnight ago.'

'I do not,' said Celia.

Ronald turned to the shoemaker and whispered to him and put something in his hand. The shoemaker rose up at once and went out. He banged the outer door shut behind him.

'Celia,' said Ronald.

'Leave me alone,' said Celia.

They sat in the growing darkness. The only light in the room was the dull glow from the range. Ronald could see the dark outline of the girl beside the fire. For ten minutes they neither moved nor spoke.

At last the door opened again and the old man came back. He groped his way to the table and put a bottle down on it. 'That's it,' he said to Ronald and laid down some loose coins beside the bottle. 'And that's the change.'

'Celia,' said Ronald, 'I'm sorry to hear you aren't well. I've got something here that'll maybe help you. A little brandy.'

'That's kind of you,' said Celia.

She picked up the poker and drove it into the black coal on top of the range. The room flared wildly with lights and shadows. The three dark figures were suddenly sitting in a warm rosy flickering world.

Celia took two cups from the cupboard and set them on the table and poured brandy into them.

'That's enough for me,' said Ronald, and put his hand over the cup next to him.

Celia filled the other cup to the top. Then she lifted it to her mouth with both hands and gulped it like water.

'Good health,' said the shoemaker. 'I'm saying that and I mean it though I'm not a drinking man myself. The very best of luck to you both.'

Ronald raised his cup and drank meagrely from it and put it down again on the table. 'Cheers,' he said.

Celia took another mouthful and set down her empty cup beside the bottle.

'Are you feeling better now, Celia?' said the shoe-maker.

'A wee bit,' said Celia. She filled up her cup again. 'I'm very glad to see you,' she said to Ronald.

'That's better,' said the shoemaker, 'that's the way to speak.'

Celia took a drink and said, 'Ronald, supposing I come to live at Clett what's going to become of Thomas?'

'I'll be all right,' said the shoemaker, 'don't worry about me. I'll manage fine.'

'He'll come and live with us,' said Ronald. 'There's plenty of room.'

'No', said Celia, 'but who's going to walk a mile and more to Clett to get their boots mended? We must think of that. He'll lose trade.'

'Don't drink so fast,' said the shoemaker.

'And besides that,' said Celia, 'he'll miss his friends, all the ones that come and visit him here and play draughts with him. What would he do without his game of draughts? Clett's a long distance away. I'm very pleased, Ronald, that you've come to see me.'

'I'm pleased to be here,' said Ronald.

'Light the lamp,' said the shoemaker happily.

'I love you both very much,' said Celia. 'You're the two people that I love most in the whole world.'

Celia filled up her cup again. This time half the brandy spilled over the table.

'I don't know whether I'll come to Clett or not,' said Celia. 'I'll have to think about it. I have responsibilities here. That's what makes me feel ill, being torn this way and that. I can't be in two places, can I? I love you both very much. I want you to know that, whatever happens.'

She suddenly started to cry. She put her hands over her face and her whole body shook with grief. She sat down in her chair beside the fire and sobbed long and bitterly.

The two men looked at each other, awed and awkward.
'I'll put a match to the lamp,' said the shoemaker.
'Then we'll see what's what.'

Celia stopped crying for a moment and said, 'Leave the
bloody lamp alone.' Then she started to sob again,
louder than ever.

Ronald got to his feet and went over to Celia. He put
his arm across her shoulder. 'Poor Celia,' he said, 'tell
me what way I can help thee?'

Celia rose to her feet and screamed at him. 'You go
away from here, you bastard,' she shouted. 'Just go
away! I want never to see you again! Clear off!'

'Celia,' pleaded the old man.

'If that's what you want, Celia,' said Ronald. He
picked up his beret from the chair and stood with his
back to the cupboard. 'Good night, Thomas,' he said.

'Come back, Ronald,' said the shoemaker. 'Celia isn't
herself tonight. She doesn't mean a word of what she
says.'

The flames were dying down in the range. Celia and
Ronald and the shoemaker moved about in the room,
three unquiet shadows.

'Good night, Celia,' said Ronald from the door.

'I hate you, you bastard,' she shrieked at him.

The last flame died. In the seething darkness the girl
and the old man heard the bang of the outer door closing.
Celia sat down in her chair and began to cry again, a slow
gentle wailing.

Half-way up the steps of the close the shoemaker
caught up with Ronald. 'This is the worst she's ever been,'
he said. 'You know the way it is with her – she drinks
heavily for a week or so, anything she can get, and then
for a month or six weeks after that she's as peaceable as
a dove. But this is the worst she's ever been. God knows
what will come of her.'

'God knows,' said Ronald.

'It started on Monday night,' said the shoemaker. 'That Norsky was here with foreign hooch.'

'Don't worry, Thomas,' said Ronald. 'It'll turn out all right, like you say.'

'She'll be fine next time you come back,' said the shoe-maker. 'Just you wait and see.'

Ronald got on to his bicycle at the head of the close.

The shoemaker went back slowly into the house. As he opened the door Celia's low voice came out of the darkness. 'God forgive me,' she was saying gently and hopelessly, 'O God forgive me.'

7

'No,' said Celia to the minister, 'I don't believe in your God. It's no good. You're wasting your time. What the Hamnavoe folk are saying is true, I'm a bad woman. I drink. Men come about the place all hours of the night. It isn't that I want them fumbling at me with their mouths and their hands. That sickens me. I put up with it for the drink they have in their pockets. I must drink.

'You're not a drinking man, Mr Blackie. I know that. I *had* to buy this bottle of wine from the licensed grocer's. It gives me courage to speak to you. Try to understand that. And we're sitting here in the half darkness because I can speak to you better in this secrecy. Faces tell lies to one another. You know the way it is. The truth gets buried under smiles.

'I drink because I'm frightened. I'm so desperately in-volved with all the weak things, lonely things, suffering things I see about me. I can't bear the pity I feel for them, not being able to help them at all. There's blood every-where. The world's a torture chamber, just a sewer of pain. That frightens me.

'Yesterday it was a gull and a water rat. They met at the end of this pier. I was pinning washing to the line when I saw it. The gull came down on the rat and swallowed it whole the way it would gulp a crust of bread, then with one flap of its wing it was out over the sea again. I could see the shape of the rat in the blackback's throat, a kind of fierce twist and thrust. The bird broke up in the air. It screamed. Blood and feathers showered out of it. The dead gull and the living rat made separate splashes in the water.

'It seems most folk can live with that kind of thing. Not me – I get all caught up in it . . .'

Stars slowly thickened and brightened in the window that looked over the harbour. The rising tide began to lap against the gable ends of the houses.

'Mr Blackie,' said Celia, 'an earthquake ruined a town in Serbia last week. The ground just opened and swallowed half the folk. Did your God in his mercy think up that too? The country folk in Viet Nam, what kind of vice is it they're gripped in, guns and lies and anger on both sides of them, a slowly tightening agony? Is your God looking after them? They never harmed anybody, but the water in the rice fields is red now all the time. Black men and white men hate each other in Chicago and Cape Town. God rules everything. He knew what was going to happen before the world was made. So we're told. If that's goodness, I have another name for it. Not the worst human being that ever lived would do the things God does. Tell me this, was God in the Warsaw ghetto too? I just want to know. I was reading about it last week in a book I got out of the Library.

'I know you don't like this darkness and the sound of wine being poured in the glass. It's the only way I can speak to you and be honest. . . .

'I remember my mother and my father. They were like

16

two rocks in the sea. Life might be smooth or rough for me – there was hunger every now and then when the fishing was poor – but the two rocks were always there. I knew every ledge and cranny. I flew between them like a young bird.

'We were poor, but closer together because of that. We gave each other small gifts. I would take shells and seapinks into the house for them. My father always had a special fish for me when he came in from the west, a codling or a flounder as small as my hand. Then my mother would bake a small bannock for me to eat with it at teatime, when I was home from school.

'I was twelve years old. One morning when I got up for school my mother was standing in the door looking out over the harbour. The fire was dead. She told me in a flat voice I wasn't to go to school that day, I was to go back to my room and draw the curtain and stay there till she called me. An hour later I heard feet on the pier. I looked through the edge of the curtain. Four fishermen were carrying something from the boat into the house. The thing was covered with a piece of sail and there was a trail of drops behind it. My father was in from his creels for the last time.

'We knew what real poverty was after that. My mother was too proud to take anything from the Poor Fund. "Of course not," she said, "my grandfather was schoolmaster in Hoy." . . . But in the middle of February she swallowed her pride and went to the Poor Inspector. One night I woke up and heard voices and came downstairs and I saw Thomas Linklater the shoemaker having supper beside the fire. A month after that my mother married him in the registry office. He came and sat in my father's chair and slept in my father's bed. He carried a new smell into our house, leather and rosin, like an animal of a different species.

'I hated him. Of course I smiled and spoke. But in my room, in the darkness, I hated the stranger.

'Three years went past. Then it was my mother's turn. I watched her changing slowly. I didn't know what the change was, nor why Dr Wilson should trouble to come so often. Then I heard Maisie Ness saying "cancer" to the watchmaker's wife at the end of the close. My mother was a good-looking woman. She was a bit vain and she'd often look long in the mirror, putting her hair to rights and smiling to her reflection. The change went on in her all that summer. She looked in the mirror less and less. Every day though she did her housework. The room had to be swept and the dishes put away before Dr Wilson called. Half a ghost, she knelt at the unlit fire and struck a match. That last morning she laid three bowls of porridge on the table. She looked at her withered face in the mirror. Then she groped for her chair and sank into it. She was dead before I could put down my spoon. The shoemaker hurried away to find Dr Wilson. The body slowly turned cold in the deep straw chair.

'I heard the shoemaker crying in his room the day before the funeral.

' "Blessed are the dead which die in the Lord" – that's what you said at the graveside. It was a poor way to die. It was ugly and degrading and unblessed, if anything ever was.

'We were alone in the house together then, a girl and an old cobbler. It was the beginning of winter. We spoke to each other only when it was needful. He gave me the housekeeping money every Friday and it was never enough. "There'll be more soon," he would say, "It's hard times, a depression all over the country. So- and-so owes five pounds for two pairs of shoes and I had a bill from the wholesale leather merchant for twenty pounds odds." . . . I wanted cakes on the table at the week-end but there was never anything but the usual bread and oat-cakes and margarine.

'Christmas came. I wanted a few decorations about the house, a tree, paper bells, some tinsel, a dozen cards to send to my special friends – you know the way it is with young girls. "We can't afford nonsense like that," the shoemaker said. "We should be thankful to God for a roof over our heads." . . . And so the walls remained bare.

'That Christmas I hated him worse than ever.

' "Celia," he said at Hogmanay, just before it struck midnight, "I'm not a drinking man. But it's bad luck not to drink a health to the house at this time of year. We'll take one small dram together."

'He brought a half-bottle of whisky out of the cupboard.

'The clock struck twelve. We touched glasses. I shuddered as the whisky went down. It burned my mouth and my stomach and it took tears to my eyes. "He's doing this deliberately to hurt me," I thought. My eyes were still wet when the door opened and Mr Spence the jeweller came in. He had a bottle of whisky in his hand to wish us a good New Year. He poured three glasses and we toasted each other. The cobbler merely wet his lips. I drank my whisky down quickly to get it over with.

'It's hard to explain what happened next. I knew who I was before I took that drink – a poor girl in an ordinary house on a fisherman's pier. I stood there holding an empty glass in my hand. A door was opening deep inside me and I looked through it into another country. I stood between the two places, confused and happy and excited. I still wore Celia's clothes but the clothes were all a disguise, bits of fancy dress, a masquerade. You know the ballad about the Scottish King who went out in the streets of Edinburgh in bonnet and tradesman's apron? I wore the clothes of a poor girl but I was wise, rich, great, gentle, good.

Then doon he let his duddies fa',
And doon he let them fa'
And he glittered a' in gold
Far abune them a'.

The world was all mine and I longed to share it with everybody. Celia was a princess in her little house on the pier. She pretended to be poor but she had endless treasures in her keeping, and it was all a secret, nobody knew about it but Celia. A wild happiness filled the house.

'I bent down and kissed the old shoemaker.

'Mr Spence, I remember, was pouring another whisky into my glass. The confusion and the happiness increased. I felt very tired then, I remember. I went to bed wrapped in silks and swan's feathers.

'It was Celia the poor girl who woke up next morning. There was a hard gray blanket up at her face. She had a mouth like ashes. The wireless when she switched it on downstairs told of people dying of hunger in the streets of Calcutta, drifting about like wraiths and lying down on the burning pavements. And a plane had fallen from the sky in Kansas and forty people were dead on a hillside.

'She cried, the poor princess, beside the dead fire.

'The next Friday out of the housekeeping money I bought a bottle of cheap wine.

'That's all there is to tell, really. You've heard the confession of an alcoholic, or part of it, for the bad fairy tale isn't over yet.

'Once a month, maybe every six weeks, the fisher girl craves for news of the lost country, the real world, what she calls her kingdom. For a week or more I enchant myself away from the town and the pier and the sound of cobbling. When I have no more money left I encourage men to come here with drink. I'm shameless about it now. Everybody who has a bottle is welcome, even Mr Snoddy.

At the end of every bout I'm in deeper exile than the time before. Every debauch kills a piece of Celia—I almost said, kills a part of her soul, but of course I don't believe in that kind of thing any more.

'And so the bad fairy tale goes on and the fisher girl who thinks that somehow she's a princess is slowly fitted with the cold blood and leathery skin and the terrible glittering eye of a toad.

'This kingdom I've had a glimpse of, though—what about that? It *seemed* real and precious. It seemed like an inheritance we're all born for, something that belongs to us by right.

'If that's true, it should be as much *there* as this pier is in the first light of morning. Why do we have to struggle towards it through fogs of drink? What's the good of all this mystery? The vision should be like a loaf or a fish, simple and real, something given to nourish the whole world.

'I blame God for that too.'

There was no sound for a while but the lapping of harbour water against stone as the tide rose slowly among the piers and slipways. The huge chaotic ordered wheel of stars tilted a little westward on its axis.

'The bottle's nearly empty,' said Celia, 'and I haven't said what I meant to say at all. I wonder if the licensed grocer would sell me another bottle? No, it's too late. And besides, I don't think I have enough money in my purse. And besides, you don't want to listen to much more of this bad talk.

'All the same, you can see now why I could never be a member of your church. All I could bring to it is this guilt, shame, grief for things that happen, a little pity, a sure knowledge of exile.

'Will Christ accept that?'

There was another longer silence in the room.

'Celia,' said the Reverend Andrew Blackie, a little hopelessly, 'you must try to have faith.'

The girl's window was full of stars. The sky was so bright that the outlines of bed and chair and cupboard could be dimly seen, and the shapes of an empty bottle and a glass on the table.

'I want to have faith,' said Celia. 'I want that more than anything in the world.'

8

Ronald Leask worked his creels with Jock Henryson all that Saturday afternoon along the west coast. They hauled eighty creels under Marwick Head and Yesnaby. In the late afternoon the wind shifted round to the north-west and strengthened and brought occasional squalls of rain. They decided to leave their remaining score of creels under the Black Crag till morning and make for home before it got dark. They had a box of lobsters and half a basket of crabs, a fair day's work. As Ronald turned the *Celia* into Hoy Sound he saw three Norwegian whalers racing for the shelter of Hamnavoe on the last of the flood tide. Another squall of rain hit them. Ronald put on his sou'wester and buttoned his black oilskin up to the chin. Jock Henryson was at the wheel now, in the shelter of the cabin.

'It's going to be a dirty night,' said Jock.

They delivered their lobsters and crabs at the Fishermen's Society pier. Then Jock said he must go home for his supper. 'You come too,' he said to Ronald. 'The wife'll have something in the pot.'

'No,' said Ronald, 'I think I'll go along for a drink.'

It was raining all the time now. The flagstones of the street shone. Ronald stopped for a few seconds at the head of the shoemaker's close, then he walked on more quickly until he came to the lighted window of the

Hamnavoe Bar. He pushed open the door. Bill MacIsaac the boatbuilder was at the bar drinking beer with Thorfinn Vik the farmer from Helliar. Sammy Flett the drunk was in too—he was half stewed and he was pestering the barman to give him a pint, and Drew the barman was refusing him patiently but firmly. A half-empty bottle of cheap wine stuck out of Sammy Flett's pocket.

'Here's Ronald Leask, a good man,' said Sammy Flett, going up to Ronald unsteadily. 'Ronald, you're a good friend of mine and I ask you to accept a cigarette out of my packet, and I'm very glad of your offer to furnish me with a glass of beer for old time's sake.'

'A glass of whisky,' said Ronald to Drew the barman.

'Absolutely delighted, old friend,' said Sammy Flett.

'It's not for you,' said Drew the barman to Sammy Flett. 'You're getting nothing, not a drop. The police sergeant was here this morning and your father with him and I know all about the trouble you're causing at home, smashing the chairs and nearly setting fire to the bed at the week-end. This place is out of bounds to you, sonny boy. I promised the sergeant and your old man. You can push off any time you like.'

'That's all lies,' said Sammy Flett. 'Just give me one pint of ordinary beer. That's not much for a man to ask.'

'No,' said Drew the barman.

'I demand to see the manager,' said Sammy Flett.

Ronald Leask drank his whisky at one go and put down his empty glass and nodded to Drew. The barman filled it up again.

'No water?' said Bill MacIsaac the boatbuilder, smiling across at Ronald.

'No,' said Ronald, 'no water.'

'Men in love,' said Thorfinn Vik of Helliar, 'don't need water in their drink.' Vik was in one of his dangerous insulting moods.

Sammy Flett went into the toilet. They heard the glug-glug of wine being drunk, then a long sigh.

The door opened and Mr William Snoddy the builder's clerk came in out of the rain. He looked round the bar nervously. 'A small whisky,' he said to Drew the barman, 'and put a little soda in it, not too much, and a bottle of export, if you please.' . . . He wiped his spectacles with his handkerchief and owled the bar with bulging naked eyes and put his spectacles on again. Then he recognized the man he was standing beside.

'Why, Ronald,' he said. 'It isn't often we see you in the bar. It's a poor night, isn't it?'

Ronald stared straight ahead at the rank of bottles under the bar clock. He put back his head and drank the remains of his second glass of whisky.

'Ronald, have a glass of whisky with me,' said Mr Snoddy, taking his wallet out of his inside pocket. 'It'll be a pleasure.'

'Same again,' said Ronald to the barman. 'And I'll pay for my own drink with my own money.'

Mr Snoddy flushed till his brow was almost as pink as his nose. Then he put his wallet back in his inside pocket.

Sammy Flett emerged from the toilet, smiling.

Bill MacIsaac and Thorfinn Vik began to play darts at the lower end of the bar.

'Oh well,' said Mr Snoddy, 'I don't suppose you can force a person to speak to you if he doesn't want to.' He drank his whisky down quickly and took a sip of beer.

Suddenly Sammy Flett came up behind Mr Snoddy and threw his arm round his neck. 'If it isn't my dear friend Mr Snoddy,' said Sammy Flett. 'Mr Snoddy, accept a cigarette, with my compliments.'

'Go away,' cried Mr Snoddy. 'Go away. Just leave me alone.'

'Mr Snoddy,' said Sammy Flett, 'I'll take the whisky

that Mr Leask refused to accept for reasons best known to himself.'

'I come in here for a quiet drink,' said Mr Snoddy to the barman, trying to disengage his neck from Sammy Flett's arm.

'And you shall have it, dear Mr Snoddy,' said Sammy Flett. 'Accompany me to the gentleman's toilet. We shall have a drink of wine together. Mr Snoddy is always welcome to have a drink from Sammy.'

'Leave Mr Snoddy alone,' said Drew the barman.

The door opened and six Norwegian fishermen came in. 'Six double scotches, six Danish lagers,' Per Bjorling said to the barman. The Norwegians shook the rain from their coats and leaned against the bar counter. A row of six blond heads shone with wetness under the lamps.

'I know what they're saying about you, Mr Snoddy,' said Sammy Flett. 'They say you're going with other women. They say you're unfaithful to Mrs Snoddy. It's an evil world and they'll say anything but their prayers. But I don't believe that, Mr Snoddy. You and me, we're old friends, and I wouldn't believe such a thing about you. Not Sammy. Never.'

Mr Snoddy looked about him, angry and confused. He left his half-empty glass standing on the counter and went out quickly, clashing the door behind him.

'Mr Snoddy is a very fine man,' said Sammy Flett to the Norwegians.

'Is so?' said one of the Norwegians, smiling.

'Yes,' said Sammy Flett, 'and he's a very clever man too.'

'Interesting,' said another Norwegian.

'I'm no fool myself,' said Sammy Flett. 'I didn't sail up Hoy Sound yesterday in a banana skin. Sammy knows a thing or two.'

Dod Isbister the plumber came in and Jimmy Gold the

postman and Andrew Thomson the crofter from Knowe. They went to the upper-end of the bar and ordered beer. They emptied a box of dominoes on the counter and began to play.

The dart players finished their game and stuck their darts in the cork rim of the board. Thorfinn Vik was a bit drunk. He came over and stood beside Ronald Leask and began to sing:

I was dancing with my darling at the Tennessee waltz
When an old friend I happened to see,
Introduced him to my sweetheart and while they were dancing
My friend stole my sweetheart from me.

'No singing,' said Drew the barman sternly. 'No singing in this bar. There's guests in the lounge upstairs.'

Thorfinn Vik turned to Ronald Leask. 'That's a song that you'll appreciate, Mr Leask,' he said. 'I sang it specially for you. A song about disappointed love.'

'Same again,' said Ronald Leask to the barman.

'A beautiful song,' said Sammy Flett from the middle of the Norwegian group. He had a glass of whisky in one hand and a glass of lager in the other that one of the whalers had bought for him. 'Very delightfully sung. Have you got songs in Norway as good as that? I daresay you have. Silence now for a Norwegian love song.'

'No singing,' said Drew.

'We sing only on our boat,' said Per Bjorling. 'We respect your rules. Please to give us seven double scotches and seven Danish lagers.' . . . To Sammy Flett he said, 'There will be singings later on the *Erika*—how you say?—a sing-song.'

'You are the true descendants of Vikings,' said Sammy Flett.

'No,' said a young Norwegian, 'they were cruel men. It is best to forget such people, no? We are peaceable fishermen.'

'Such is truthfully what we are,' said another Norwegian.

The door opened quietly and Mr Spence the jeweller tiptoed in. He shook his umbrella close and went up to the bar. 'One half-bottle of the best whisky, to carry out,' he murmured to Drew the barman. He laid two pound notes discreetly on the counter.

'Mr Spence,' cried Sammy Flett from the centre of the Norwegian group. 'My dear friend.'

'Leave Mr Spence alone,' said Drew. 'He doesn't want anything about you.'

'I am content where I am', said Sammy Flett, 'in the midst of our Scandinavian cousins. But there's nothing wrong in greeting my old friend Mr Spence.'

Mr Spence smiled and picked up his change and slid the half-bottle into his coat pocket.

'I think I know where you're off to with that,' said Sammy Flett, wagging a finger at him.

Mr Spence smiled again and went out as quietly and quickly as he had come in.

'Yes,' said Thorfin Vik of Helliar, 'we all know where he's going. . . .' He winked across at the domino players. 'Mr Leask knows too.'

'I want no trouble in here,' said Drew the barman.

'Same again,' said Ronald Leask and pushed his empty glass at the barman. His face was very red.

'Is clock right?' said Per Bjorling.

'Five minutes fast,' said Drew. 'It's twenty minutes to ten.'

Sammy Flett drank first his whisky and then his lager very quickly. The huge adams-apple above his dirty collar wobbled two or three times. He sighed and said,

'Sammy is happy now. Sammy asks nothing from life but a wee drink now and then.'

'I am happy for you,' said the Norwegian boy. 'I will now buy you other drink.'

'No,' said Sammy Flett, 'not unless you all promise to partake of a little wine with me later in the gentlemen's toilet. At closing time Sammy will show you the pleasures of Hamnavoe. Sammy knows all the places.'

'Here is pleasures enough,' said the oldest Norwegian, 'in the pub.'

'No,' said Sammy, 'but I will take you to girls.'

'Girls,' said the old man. 'Oh no no. I am grandfather.'

'I have little sweetheart outside of Hammerfest,' said the boy. 'Gerd. She is milking the cattles and makes butter, also cheese from goats.'

'Also I am married,' said another Norwegian, 'and also is Paal and Magnus and Henrik. No girls. All are committed among us but Per.'

'Is true,' said Per Bjorling gravely.

'Per is liberty to find a girl where he likes,' said the old man. 'Per is goodlooking, is handsome, there is no trouble that Per our skipper will find a beautiful girl.'

The other Norwegians laughed.

'He's like a film star,' said Sammy Flett. 'Thank you most kindly, I'll have a glass of whisky and a bottle of beer. No offence. Per has a profile like a Greek hero.'

'Has found a beautiful girl already,' said the boy, smiling, 'in Hamnavoe.'

'One bottle of vodka,' said Per Bjorling to Drew, 'for outside drinking.'

Drew the barman took down a bottle of vodka from the shelf and called out, 'Last orders, gentlemen.'

'Double whisky,' said Ronald Leask.

Sammy Flett said to Per Bjorling, 'Are you going to visit this young lady now with your bottle of vodka?'

'A gift to her,' said Per Bjorling. 'Is a good girl. Is kind. Is understanding, intelligent. I like her very much.'

'What is the name of this fortunate young lady, if I might make so bold as to ask?' said Sammy Flett. 'Listen, Ronald. Per Bjorling is just going to tell us the name of his Hamnavoe sweetheart.'

Per Bjorling said, 'Celia.'

For about five seconds there was no sound in the bar but the click of dominoes on the counter.

Then Ronald Leask turned and hit Per Bjorling with his fist on the side of the head. The lager glass fell from Per Bjorling's hand and smashed on the floor. The force of the blow sent him back against the wall, his hands up at his face. He turned to Ronald Leask and said, 'Is not my wish to cause offence to any man present.'

'Cut it out,' cried Drew the barman. 'That's enough now.'

Ronald Leask stepped forward and hit Per Bjorling again, on the mouth. A little blood ran down Per Bjorling's jaw and his cap fell on the floor. He turned and hit Ronald Leask in the stomach and Ronald Leask flapped against the counter like a shiny black puppet. A score of glasses fell and smashed and a rapid pool of whisky and beer formed on the floor. Ronald Leask and Per Bjorling splintered and splashed through it, wrestling with each other. Ronald Leask clubbed down his fist on Per Bjorling's eye and Per Bjorling thrashed him across the jaw with the back of his hand. Ronald Leask went down on all fours among the beer and the broken glass.

'I am sorry for this,' said Per Bjorling and held out his hand.

Ronald Leask got slowly to his feet. His trouser knees were sopping wet and the palms of his hands cut and bleeding. A small bubble of blood grew and burst at his right nostril.

'Get out of here,'said Drew the barman, taking Ronald Leask by the sleeve of his oilskin, 'and never come back again. That applies to you too,' he said to Per Bjorling.

'So this is your Scotch hospitality,' said the Norwegian called Paal, 'to strike a man without reason. This we will not forget.'

'Remember this too,' said Thorfinn Vik, and struck Paal on the ear. 'This is our bar where we come to enjoy ourselves and this is our town and our women live in it.'

Drew picked up the telephone and his forefinger juggled in the dial.

'This is cowardice,' said the Norwegian boy. He stepped forward and took Thorfinn Vik by the throat. They lurched violently, locked together, between the seats and the bar counter. Half a dozen more glasses went over and smashed. Bill MacIsaac the boatbuilder tried to prise Thorfinn Vik and the young Norwegian apart. Andrew Thomson of Knowe put down his dominoes and began to take off his jacket slowly. 'I don't like fighting,' he said, 'but I'll fight if there's fighting to be done.'

'Gentlemen, gentlemen,' piped Sammy Flett from the fringe of the fight. Then he noticed an unattended glass of whisky on the bar counter and made for it. He was hidden behind a welter of heaving backs.

'You are bad man,' said the old Norwegian to Ronald Leask and slapped him magisterially across the face.

'Enough,' cried Per Bjorling.

Two policemen stood in the door.

Dod Isbister with a bottle in his hand and the Norwegian called Magnus with a glass in his hand were circling each other at the top end of the bar. Ronald Leask lashed out at Paal with his foot and missed and kicked Henrik on the elbow. Thorfinn Vik and the young Norwegian went over on the floor with a thud that made the bottles reel and rattle and clink. Dod Isbister threw the bottle he was holding and it missed Magnus's head and smashed into the lamp bulb. The light went out. The pub was a twilight full of grunting, breathing, slithering, cursing shadows.

'All right, gentlemen,' said the voice of Drew the barman, 'you can break it up. The law is here.'

The two policemen beamed their torches slowly over the wreckage. The fighters disengaged themselves. One by one they got to their feet.

'So this is the way it is,' said the sergeant. 'You'll have to come along to the station. We have accommodation for gentry like you. You haven't heard the last of this, I'm afraid. The sheriff will be wanting to see you all next Tuesday.'

'Not me, sergeant,' said Sammy Flett. 'Sammy never laid a finger on anybody.'

'You too,' said the sergeant. 'I wouldn't be surprised if you weren't at the bottom of this, Flett.'

Later, in the Black Maria going to the police station, Sammy Flett said, 'That was the best fight since the Kirkwall men threw Clarence Shaw into the harbour last carnival week.'

'Shut up, drunkard,' said Thorfinn Vik sleepily from the corner of the van.

'No, Thorfinn,' said Sammy Flett,' but I want to re-assure everyone, especially our Norwegian guests. The beds in the lock-up are very comfortable. The sergeant's wife will give us a cup of tea and toast in the morning. I know, because I've had bed and breakfast at Her Majesty's expense on twenty-two occasions—no, this makes it twenty-three. Everybody is very nice.'

'The little Gerd,' said the young Norwegian miserably. 'I am thinking of her so very much.'

The Black Maria jolted to a stop. They had arrived.

In the shoemaker's room the lamp was turned down low. It threw a feeble pool of light in one corner. The shoemaker was in his iron bed; he leaned back on three pillows and struggled for breath. Every inhalation was hard-won and shallow; the slack strings of his throat grew taut to force a passage for it, and his whole torso laboured to expel it again. His breathing slowly thickened and roughened, came in a quick spasm, and then he turned over on the pillows in a storm of feeble importunate coughing.

Celia came quickly through from the other room. She sat down on the edge of the bed and took the shoemaker's damp hand in both hers. 'You'll be all right,' she said. 'Just take it easy.'

The coughing stopped and the old man lay back on his pillows with his mouth open. Celia wiped his face with her apron. Then she lifted a small brown bottle from the table and shook a tablet out and poured some water in a cup. 'You've to take a tablet every four hours, Dr Wilson says,' she said. 'It stops the coughing.' She put the tablet in his mouth and raised his head and gave him a sip of water.

'If only I could sleep,' whispered the shoemaker. He lay back on the pillows with his eyes shut. 'I'm a very poor old sick man.'

'I won't leave you,' said Celia.

'Tell me one thing,' said the shoemaker, 'then maybe I can get to sleep. Is there any man or drink in the room next door?'

'No,' said Celia.

'Tell me the truth,' he whispered sternly. 'The truth, mind. I heard someone at the door.'

'Snoddy came at half-past eight,' said Celia. 'I sent him

away. I told him you were ill. What's more, I told him I didn't want his drink.'

'Till the next time,' said the shoemaker.

'I suppose so,' said Celia.

The shoemaker's breath slowly roughened as new threads of phlegm spun themselves into a thick cord in his chest. Then suddenly he was possessed by spasm after spasm of futile coughing. He drew himself up in the bed and Celia put her arms round his thin body and held him close to her until the tough cord of phlegm broke and the coughing stopped. She took a bowl from the bedside chair and he managed to spit into it. The effort exhausted him. Celia laid him back on his pillows. Then she wiped his face in her apron.

'If only I could sleep,' said the shoemaker. 'I was dropping off to sleep an hour and more ago and then I was wakened first by Snoddy and then by a terrible noise along the street.'

'There was fighting in the Hamnavoe Bar,' said Celia. 'So Snoddy said. That's what you heard. Drew had to get the police.'

'It sounded like an earthquake,' said the shoemaker.

Celia stroked his chest outside his gray flannel shirt. 'Try to sleep now,' she said. 'I'll stay beside you till you go to sleep.' . . . After a time she felt his chest grow quiet under her hand. His eyes were shut and his breath came deep and even through slightly parted lips. Celia knew that he wasn't asleep, but he was pretending to sleep so that she could get back to her bed.

Outside the rain slanted darkly. A sudden gust of wind caught the downpour and threw it against the window till all the panes surged and throbbed. Through the onset Celia heard a discreet tapping at the outside door.

'Don't let him in,' said the shoemaker, opening his eyes.

It was Mr Spence the jeweller. 'Celia,' he said.

'The old man isn't well,' said Celia in a low voice. 'The doctor was here in the afternoon. I'll have to be up with him all night.'

'Perhaps if I could just come in,' said Mr Spence.

'No,' said Celia.

'I'm very wet, my dear,' said Mr Spence.

'Please go home,' said Celia, 'Please.'

Mr Spence took the flask of whisky from his coat pocket. 'We will just have one little toddy,' he said. 'Thomas won't mind me being in the house. He tells me I can come whenever I like. You know that. A little dram for a damp night, eh?'

'Not tonight,' said Celia, 'I'm sorry.'

The rain slanted all about Mr Spence, a diagonal bright-dark nagging susurration on the flagstones of the pier. The gutters bubbled. Celia could smell the wetness from his clothes.

'Celia,' said Mr Spence in a hurt voice, 'I am a very lonely man.'

'Everyone is lonely,' said Celia gently. 'We're all prisoners. We must try to find out a way to be pardoned.'

She shut the door and drew the bar across it. She was just about to turn into her own seaward room when she heard the shoemaker speaking aloud to himself in the room with the dim light and the noise of rain in it. She stood in the lobby and listened.

'And so it'll be all right once we're settled in Clett. Ronald has a small room I can bide in. It doesn't matter about me, I won't live that long. But Celia, she'll be happy at last. She'll soon learn to look after the cow and the few hens, yes, he'll get a pot of soup when he comes in cold from the fishing. She'll be a good wife to Ronald. And I tell you this, Ronald won't allow all them bottles in his cupboard, no, and no bloody foreigners'll get within a stone's throw of the place, and as for Snoddy, the dog of Clett'll tear the arse off the likes of him. Mr Spence, he can come as usual twice a week for a game of draughts, I'm sure Ronald won't object to that. We'll be fine once we're settled in Clett. Not that Ronald Leask's conferring any favour on Celia, not a bit of it, he's a lucky chap to be getting the likes of Celia for a wife. She can cook and sew and wash as well as any woman in Hamnavoe. I'll maybe be a burden to them for a winter or two, but Ronald said I could come, and by that time they'll likely have another burden, a bairn in the cradle, but a sweet burden, not an old done man. Once Celia's settled in Clett she'll have a new life entirely, there'll be no more drink and no more poverty and no more stray men in the night. An end to this darkness.'

Celia went softly into the room. The shoemaker closed his eyes quickly and pretended to be asleep. But another rope of phlegm was beginning to rasp in his chest. There was a smell too, all about the bed. Celia sat beside him and wiped his face with her apron. He opened his eyes and said, 'I'm sorry. I think I've messed the bed up.' He was ashamed and his eyes were wet.

'I know,' said Celia. 'Don't worry. I'll get you cleaned up before anything else. There's a kettle of hot water on the range. Plenty of clean sheets in the cupboard.'

She opened the window to let the smell out. Rain and wind swirled in and the shoemaker began to cough. She closed the window again quickly.

For the next twenty minutes Celia washed the old man and dried him and put a clean shirt on him and stripped the bed and put clean sheets on it and set the soiled stinking sheets in a tub of disinfected water in the lobby.

'You'll feel better now,' said Celia. 'I'm going to make a cup of tea for the two of us.'

The shoemaker was racked with a violent spasm of

coughing. She held him till the tough cord of phlegm shore in his throat and he spat it out. She laid him back exhausted on the pillows.

'Fighting along the street a while ago,' said the shoemaker wearily. 'It's always them foreigners.'

'It's all quiet now,' said Celia. 'Time you had another tablet though.'

She took a yellow tablet out of the bottle on to her hand and put it on his tongue. She laid her arm round his shoulders and raised him and put the cup of water to his mouth.

'They don't seem to help me, them tablets,' said the shoemaker.

'They will,' said Celia. 'Give them time. Dr Wilson's tablets always work, you know that.'

'Maybe I'll get a sleep now,' said the shoemaker.

'Try,' said Celia.

But the hoarseness was in his chest again. He coughed and spat out thick phlegm. But as always when this sickness was on him, he had hardly torn the purulent fungus from his bronchial tree when a new growth rose about it, blocking and strangling his breath.

'I'm a terrible nuisance to you,' he said, 'a silly awkward old man.'

'You're not,' said Celia, 'and you'll be better tomorrow. And there's a fine shed at Clett where you can mend boots. I'll ask Ronald to put a stove in it.'

The shoemaker was suddenly asleep, the way sleep comes to the very young and the very old. His cheeks flushed like two withered apples. He breathed as quietly as a child.

'Thank God,' said Celia.

She drew the blankets up to his chin and kissed him on the forehead.

The window paled with the end of the night.

CELIA

The rain had stopped, as it often does before dawn. Celia closed the door of the shoemaker's room softly and unbarred the outer door and went out on to the pier. The first seagulls were screaming along the street, scavenging in the bins. She breathed the clean air of early morning. She stood at the pier wall and watched the sea moving darkly against the weeded steps and slipways. A rat in the seaweed squinnied at her and twitched its whiskers and went into the water with a soft plop. The sun had not yet risen, but light was assembling in broken colours over the Orphir hills. The first blackbird in the fuchsia bush under the watchmaker's wall faltered into song and then was silent again. Celia could see the boats in the harbour now and at the farm across the harbour black ploughed squares among green grass and brown heather. It would be a beautiful morning.

Then the sun rose clear of the Orphir hills and folded the girl in the light of a new day.

A Time to Keep

1

W E came down through the fields, Ingi and I.

The wedding was still going on in her father's house in Osmundwall, ten miles over the hill.

There were lacings of snow across the valley and the upper hills were white.

We saw our house in front of us, a clean new house of sea-washed stones. There was no earth-weathering on the walls yet. I had built the house myself between harvest and Christmas. Fires had been lit to burn the dampness out of it, but there was no fire yet for food and companionship. Beside the dwelling-house were byre and barn and stable that the mason had built the winter before. The thatch on the four roofs was new springy heather, covered with wire-netting and weighted with stones.

Ingi went alone into the house. I went into the byre to see that the two cows were all right. There was a sheep here and a sheep there on the field above, seven sheep in all on the hill. One sheep wandered across a line of snow, gray against white.

A new plough leaned against the wall of the barn. The blacksmith must have delivered it that afternoon. I took it inside, a gray powerful curve.

This was our croft, Ingi's and mine. I turned back towards the house. Blue smoke was rising from the roof now. The first true fire had been lit.

2

I was in the firth most days that month, though it was winter. My boat was new also. I had made her with my

38

own hands in the month of June, the dry bright month
when work can be carried on late into the night, after the
croft work is over. I called the boat *Susanna* after the
laird's wife, a red-faced generous woman. I thought a
name like that would bring us luck.

I generally got up as soon as it was light. I left Ingi in
our bed and I ate a piece of bannock and drank a mouthful
of ale. Then I put on my sea-boots and my woollen cap
and went down to the beach.

The other crofters who were fishermen also were always there before me that winter, and they kept apart
from me. I was like a stranger in the valley.

I launched *Susanna* alone. I rowed her out into the
firth alone. I set my lines alone. I didn't feel the need of
anyone except Ingi.

That winter the other crofter-fishermen avoided me.
Neither the old ones nor the young unmarried ones came
near me. They had liked me well enough the summer before but now, since the marriage, I was, it seemed, un-
popular. The men of Two-Waters especially kept to their
own side of the bay.

I fished alone.

And alone I carried the haddocks up over the fields to
the croft. Always the smoke was rising out of the roof,
sometimes gray smoke, sometimes blue, sometimes
black. But the flame beat in the hearth, the house was
alive. And always when I reached the door Ingi stood
there before me.

3

One night there was a storm from the south. None of
the boats was in the firth next morning. The clouds
pressed on the face of the hills and it was too wet to
plough, though it was the time of ploughing.

I lay long in the box-bed, my face to the wall. Ingi was up soon after it was light.

I heard her going about her work. Her poker stirred a new flame out of the embers in the hearth. The door opened. She came in with her apron full of peats. The door opened again. Now she was carrying pails of new water from the burn. They rang like bells as she set them down on the flagstones. She turned some fish that were smoking in the chimney. Then her small fists beat on the table as she kneaded the dough. She poured water into a black pot. And the door kept slamming against the wall as she went out and in, louder because of the storm. 'For God's sake,' I said, 'be quiet.'

I fell asleep for a while then.

When I woke up the storm was still prowling about the house. But the door was shut tight and the house was warm and full of the smells of new bannocks and boiled fish.

'Get up,' Ingi said, 'or we'll eat up everything, the dog and myself. You've been sleeping a night and a day.' She said a small quiet prayer over the food.

Ingi and I sat at the table and ate. She had not yet learned to cook properly—the fish was raw and the bannocks full of soda. She had been busy at more than food while I was sleeping. The stone floor was still half wet from her scrubbing and she had tried to mend the four broken creels with twine. Ingi was not a valley girl. She had spent her life behind the counter of her father's shop in Osmundwall, but she was doing her best to please me. It grew dark while we were eating.

Ingi put down her bread and took a box of matches from the mantelpiece and lit the paraffin lamp. The flame came up squint—she still didn't know how to trim a wick.

We dipped the last of our bread in the fish brew. 'I

hope this gale doesn't last,' said Ingi. 'Our fish is nearly done.'

The flame sank in the hearth.

'Tomorrow,' said Ingi, 'I will make ale, though I've never made it before. There isn't much malt left either. And I'll tell you what I need badly, a pair of black shoes for the kirk on Sundays.'

I rose from my chair and blew out the lamp.

Outside the storm prowled between the sea and the hills, restless as a beast.

Ingi put a black peat over the red embers so that the fire would stay alive till morning.

We leaned towards each other then and kissed in the darkness.

4

I dug out a new field at the side of the house—because no-one on God's earth could plough such a wilderness—and all the while I was tearing up stones and clumps of heather I thought to myself, 'What a fool! Sure as hell the laird will raise your rent for this day's work.' And my spade rang against stones or sank with a squelch into a sudden bit of bog.

I looked up once and saw a dozen women trooping across the fields to the school.

It was Good Friday.

I looked up another time and saw a horseman riding between the hills. It was the laird. He turned his horse towards the school also. The Easter service was being held there.

Two of my lambs had been born dead that morning. They lay, red bits of rag, under the wall. I would bury them afterwards.

There was one stone in the new field that just showed

a gray curve through the heather. I took the biggest hammer in the barn and was an hour breaking it up and tearing the sharp bits out of the ground.

That was enough labour for one day. The sun was going down. I turned for home.

Ingi was not in. The house was dead. The pot sat black upon a black fire. My shoulders ached with the misery and foolishness of increasing my own rent. I was very hungry too.

Ingi was at the service with the laird and the other women, listening to the story of the lash and the whins and the nails and the last words. All the women were there sitting before the missionary with open mouths, listening to that fairy tale. I and a few others in the island knew better. Mr Simpson, B.Sc., from Glasgow had not been our schoolmaster four winters for nothing.

I spent the rest of that day in the ale-house with half a dozen other ploughmen.

And how I got home to the croft again I do not know. I woke up in the morning on the rack of my own bed, with all my clothes on.

There was a jam jar with new daffodils in it in the window.

Ingi heard my awakening, a groan and a creak.

She rose up quickly from the chair where she was peeling potatoes and put her cold hand on my forehead. 'You'll be fine now,' she said. 'Bella had two lambs in the night, such bonny peedie things! Your throat must be dry. I'll get you some water.'

Bella was the old ewe. None of her lambs, so I had been told when I bought her, ever died.

'You listen to me,' I said to Ingi. 'You spend too much money every Wednesday at that grocery van. Don't you buy any more jars of jam, and sponge cakes from the bakehouse in Hamnavoe. We're poor people. Remember that.'

The daffodils in the window were like a dozen old women shawled in brightness.

The fire burned high in the hearth and the kettle sang.

I closed my eyes.

5

The old field was ploughed and the new field was completely drained and dug. When I turned for home gray smoke was rising over the chimney-head.

There were eleven sheep on the hill now and three cattle in the field, the two cows and a small black bull calf. I went into the house and Ingi was emptying the new ale out of the kirn into stone jars. 'You'll bide at home after this,' Ingi said. 'No more of that ale-house.'

But the stuff was flat. She hadn't yet mastered the craft of brewing. Until she did I would have to keep visiting the ale-house.

One day I would come in from the firth with lobsters and another day with haddocks. I got two huge halibut one morning that I could hardly carry up over the fields. She was ready with the stone jar of salt and the knife in the threshold.

I walked between the hills to pay the rent on term day. 'You've broken out land,' said the factor, 'and therefore I think it only fair you should pay ten shillings more rent come Martinmas. Furthermore you have no right to graze sheep on the hill without permission from the laird, who is not giving his permission this year. See to it.'

'Did you never hear of the Crofters' Act of 1888?' I said.

He gave me a black look. Then he licked a stamp and thudded it on the receipt and signed his name across it. 'You'll be hearing from the lawyer in Hamnavoe,' he said.

I had more kindness than usual from Ingi when I got back from that interview.

And every Sabbath she would be at the holy meeting with the old women. She was away all morning, while I sat at home reading *The Martyrdom of Man*, one of the six books in the cupboard (not counting the bible). And after the service she would come in at the door and sit in her black clothes in the chair at the other side of the fire and she would say, 'We should be very thankful.' . . . 'But,' she said one Sunday, 'my shoes are not fit to be seen in God's house.'

We were at the peat cutting a whole day that month. We came home stung with clegs, blistered by the sun, and too sore to eat or to make love. But one thing was sure: the red heart of the house would beat all next winter, for we had a great hoard of peats scattered over the hillside to dry. Ingi kissed me once and then I went to sleep in the chair till morning.

I sowed the field with oats. Then I went home in the twilight to bread and ale and the warm fire. There was a little improvement in her brewing, but still the stuff was too thick and sweet.

One morning Ingi was very sick.

6

I was sorting my catch on the beach and so were all the other fishermen when Peter of Two-Waters walked across the stones to me. John and Howie his two sons were behind him. Anna his daughter hovered in the background. 'You hauled some of my lobster creels,' Peter of Two-Waters said.

'I did not,' I said.

'Under the Kame you hauled a dozen lobster creels belonging to me,' said Peter of Two-Waters.

'That's not true,' I said.

'Don't do it again,' said Peter of Two-Waters. 'That's thieving. In Kirkwall there's a court and a sheriff and a jail.'

'I'm not a thief,' I said, 'but you're a liar.'

'Don't call my father a liar,' said John of Two-Waters. 'If you call my father a liar again I'll smash you. I will.'

'Careful,' said Howie of Two-Waters to John. Howie had always been my friend. We had sat together at the same desk in the school and afterwards we had fished to-gether a few times and we had got drunk in each other's company in the ale-house. 'Careful now,' said Howie to his brother.

'Somebody has been hauling my creels,' said old Peter of Two-Waters. 'There'll be trouble unless it stops.'

'I fish my own lobsters,' I said.

Then I put my basket of fish on my shoulder and walked home.

The truth is, I had good catches of lobster that sum-mer, and I shipped them to Billingsgate and got good money for them. I was at home on the sea. Everything I did there was right.

The men of Two-Waters, on the other hand, were poor fishermen. They were good enough crofters but old women could have fished better. They should never have gone on the sea. They hardly knew the bow of a yawl from the stern. The weather made them nervous too—they kept near the shore if there was one cloud in the sky or a whisper of wind.

'No,' said Ingi when I got home, 'you are not a thief. But don't get into any fights. That Howie of Two-Waters is so strong, he could kill an ox. Besides that, Anna of Two-Waters is my best friend in this valley, and I don't want there to be any trouble between us. This valley is too small for bad blood.'

She blew up the fire to heat a pot of ale. Then she knelt and drew off my sea boots.

7

I was baiting a line with mussels at the end of the house when I saw the black car coming between the hills and stopping where the road ended at the mouth of the valley. It was the first car ever seen in the island, a Ford.

A small, neat man with a beard and a watch-chain across his belly got out and came stepping briskly up our side of the valley.

'Ingi,' I shouted, 'your father's here.'

She was baking, going between the table, the cupboard, and the fire, a blue reek all about her.

But now all thought of bread was forgotten. She let out a cry of distress. She threw off her mealy apron, she filled a bowl of water and dipped face and hands in it and wiped herself dry with the towel. She put the text straight on the wall. She covered my six rationalist books with a cloth. She fell to combing her hair and twisting it into a new bright knot at the back of her head. All the same, the house was full of the blue hot reek of baking. And the bed was unmade. And there was a litter of fish-guts and crab toes about the door. She tried hard, Ingi, but she was not the tidiest of the croft women.

Ingi came and stood at the door.

As for me, I went on with my lines. I was not beholden to him.

Mr Sinclair, merchant in Osmundwall – and forby kirk elder, Justice of the Peace, chairman of the district council – stood at the corner of the barn.

'Father,' said Ingi.

'My girl,' said Mr Sinclair. He touched her gently on the arm.

'Well, Bill,' he said to me.

'Well,' I said.

'Father, I'm glad to see you,' said Ingi.

'No happier than I am to see you,' said Mr Sinclair. 'Ingi,' said he, 'you're not looking well. Not at all well. What way is it that we haven't seen you for three whole months, eh? Ingi, I doubt you're working too hard, is that it?'

'On a croft,' I said, 'everybody must work.'

'Is that so, Bill?' said Mr Sinclair. 'Maybe so. At the present moment I'm speaking to Ingi, to my daughter. I'll be wanting to speak to you later, before I go.'

'Say what you have to say now,' I said, 'for I have work to do.'

'Bill,' said Ingi unhappily.

'Work to do, is that it, work to do,' said Mr Sinclair. 'Then if you have so much work to do, why don't you give my daughter enough money for her to live on? Eh? Just answer me. Why don't you do that? Last month you cut down on her money. The van man told me. She couldn't buy jam or paraffin. Don't imagine I don't hear things.'

'Father,' said Ingi, 'Please.'

'We have debts,' I said, 'to the mason for the barn and to the fishmonger for twine and oilskins and to the dealer in Hamnavoe for the seven sheep and the two cows. The laird, your friend and fellow elder, is threatening to raise our rent. There was furniture and implements to pay for.'

'You and Ingi had a hundred pounds from me the week before you married,' said Mr Sinclair quietly. 'One hundred pounds sterling, a cheque for that amount.'

'You'll get it back,' I said, 'every penny.'

'Bill,' said Ingi. 'Father.'

'It was a present,' said Mr Sinclair, 'to see my daughter through her first year or two in comfort. Yes, in the kind of comfort she was used to before she came to this place. Ingi is not a strong girl. She needs looking after.'

'All the same,' I said, 'you'll be paid back. Ingi and I, we don't want your money.'

'I think we should go inside,' said Mr Sinclair. 'The whole valley's listening to what we say.'

It was true enough. A half-dozen old women were at the end of their houses, waiting like hens for scraps of scandal.

'Let them listen,' I said. 'The truth never hurt anybody.'

'Yes, come inside, *please*,' said Ingi.

'No,' I said. 'Can't you see I'm working? I must bait this line and get the boat out before the tide turns.'

'Very well,' said Mr Sinclair, 'the truth as you say will bear hearing wherever it's uttered. There are other matters to be discussed besides.'

Ingi went inside, covering her eyes with the new apron she had put on in honour of her father's arrival. From time to time I could hear a slow hard sob from inside the house.

'For example,' Mr Sinclair said, 'it has come to my ears that hardly a night passes but you're in the ale-house. Hardly a night. Yes. The ale-house. But when are you seen at the Sunday service? Never once. No, but in the ale-house when you have a few drams in you there's nothing too vile for you to say against God and his holy bible. I did not think I was marrying my daughter to a drunkard and an atheist.'

I went on baiting my line. I could hear Ingi crying continuously inside the house.

'Listen to her, the poor girl,' said Mr Sinclair. 'She does well to cry. For Ingibiorg Sinclair was a happy girl before she met up with the likes of you. She was that. And look at the shame and the misery and the poverty you've brought on her. I got her letter. She's a very unhappy girl.'

I opened a few more mussels with my knife.

'I've come here today,' he said, 'to take her home where she'll be looked after.'

I never answered.

I heard him stumping into the house. I went on with the baiting. Coil by coil the haddock line was baited. They spoke low and urgently to each other inside. Ten minutes passed. The half-dozen old women still stood at the end of the crofts. I opened a score of mussels and threw the empty blue shells on the grass among the buttercups. The gulls that had been standing along the shore all morning stirred themselves and rose seawards in tumult upon tumult of yelling circles. Down at the rock Howie of Two-Waters was stowing his creels on board. (The fool—it was not a lobster day.) I heard the door opening and a small sob out of Ingi and the brisk feet of Mr Sinclair on the threshold.

'You haven't heard the last of this,' he shouted to me.

'There's never an end to anything,' I said, 'and it's a fine morning for the haddocks.'

I waited till I heard the black Ford coughing among the hills and all the old women were inside and the last hook was baited and coiled. Then I rose and went in through the door.

Ingi sat among the half-baked bannocks, dabbing her eyes.

'Ingi,' I said, 'here's what you're going to get, a pair of new black shoes and a coat and a hat for the kirk on Sabbath. We're going to Hamnavoe on the Saturday boat, the two of us, to the shops.'

8

A new wave fell into the *Susanna* and kept the score of dying haddocks alive.

I was trying to get home before the day got worse.

It had been a fine morning. I had left Ingi in bed before the sun rose and eaten my bannock and ale standing. Then I put on thigh boots and put the oilskin over my arm.

There was sun and a blue sea when I got to the beach. The other fishermen were there too, busy around their boats. 'First the haddocks,' I said to myself, 'then the lobsters as I come home in the afternoon.'

The gulls encouraged us, white congregations drifting out in the firth, circling and dipping and crying.

I set a line and looked back at the valley. It was like a green open hand among the hills. The cliffs stood near and far, red, gray, black. In the valley chimneys began to smoke, one of them mine. Ingi was up. A green offering hand, our valley, corn-giver, fire-giver, water-giver, keeper of men and beasts. The other hand that fed us was this blue hand of the sea, which was treacherous, which had claws to it, which took more than ever it gave. Today it was peaceable enough. Blue hand and green hand lay together, like praying, in the summer dawn.

I drew in a score of haddocks, middling things.

I felt hungry after that, and had a few corn-beef sandwiches and a flask of milk.

Time for the lobsters.

I found myself drifting among three strange boats. They were Highland fishermen, from Sutherlandshire on the opposite shore of the firth. They shouted to me in Gaelic. I shook my head. One of them waved a bottle of whisky. 'This will be a language that you will be understanding,' he said in English. We drifted together. I took the bottle and had a dram. 'Another,' they said. Once more bottle and head tilted at their different angles and my throat burned. 'Ah,' said an old Highlandman, 'but you Orkneymen are terrible ones for the strong drink. Tell me,' he said, 'are they still making whisky up among the Orkney hills?' 'A few,' I said, 'but it's dangerous.' 'Ah, now,' said the old man, 'that is the real whisky, water of life, and could a man get that stuff to drink every day from the day of his weaning he would live forever.' 'I drank it once,' I said, 'and it nearly killed me.' 'People are made different,' said the old man; 'to me now it is like mother's milk.'

'I wish, however,' said a young red-headed man, 'that you Orkneymen would stay more to your own side of the firth and not poach in our waters.' 'The sea is free,' I said. 'No,' said another tall man, 'but you take our fish.' This last man who had spoken was drunk and I didn't care for the look of him, the black smoulder in his eyes when he spoke to me. 'Just as,' he went on, 'in the old days you Orkneymen came to our place and took our sheep away and were a trouble to our women. . . .' Then he said something in Gaelic which I took to be an insult. Some of the other fishermen laughed. The old man held up his hand and said, 'That is an old story that should be forgotten. It is true enough, God made the sea for all men and he created all men to be brothers. There should be no more talk of sheep and women.' . . . He offered the whisky bottle for the third time. 'No,' I said, 'for I must be getting to the lobsters now.' 'You will drink,' said the old man sharply, and I saw at once that I had offended his peace-offering. I drank a third mouthful. My body glowed like a banked-up fire. 'You will get no lobsters this day,' said the young red-headed fisherman, 'for the storm. You will be the lucky one if you manage to save your creels at all.' I looked round. The delicate egg-shell blue sky was gray as oysters, purple as mussels, and the sun slid through thickening clouds like a wan pearl. 'May God bring us safely through this bad weather and all tempests whatever,' said the old one, 'each one to the safety of his own home.' 'Amen,' spat out the tall vicious one. And at that moment the wind struck us.

All the boats turned for home.

I steered the *Susanna* through rising seas. I felt very brave on account of the Gaelic whisky. I might have been a bit frightened otherwise, for I had never been out in such seas.

I left the lobster creels under the crag and steered straight home. The lobster creels would have to wait until tomorrow, if there were any of them left at all.

The crags gathered round the *Susanna* like ghosts. She lurched and wallowed through the shallower waters. And there, through veils of rain and spindrift, I saw the beach and a solitary woman standing on it. The other boats were in a while ago. The shawled woman stood with the protective hills all round her. The valley offered her to me, Ingi, a figure still as stone. And the savage glad hand of the sea thrust me towards her.

9

Sheepay oatfield was the first to ripen. We went there with our scythes and we cut the oatfield in a day. The field was too steep for the reaper to operate. The women of Sheepay made a supper for us in the evening, as much ale and cheese and bannocks as we could eat. It was very hot in the valley that day. The men worked bare to the waist.

Then Hawkfall barley took the burnish. The field was steep also and right on the top of high crags. Gannets circled under the circling scythes. It was a rather thin crop but it was dark before the last of it was cut. 'The old man of Hawkfall shouldn't have opened that bottle of rum in the middle of the morning,' said Jeremiah of Whalerest, 'and in the hot sun too. It slowed us up. . . .' We had a sleepy supper of oatcakes and ale at Hawkfall.

The good weather held. The third morning the widow

of Girss was at every door before daybreak screeching that her oats were ready. We cut her half-acre with the reaper before dinner-time. There was no drink at Girss, neither whisky nor ale, for she was a very religious woman. But she was generous with her bread and slices of mutton. We must have eaten half a sheep. And in the heat her buttermilk tasted better than any beer.

Still the rain kept off. Two-Waters's oats that had been green the day before echoed the sunlight next morning. Peter of Two-Waters, cap in hand, stood in my door. 'We would be pleased,' said the old man, 'if you would help in our field.' 'Get the lobsters to help you,' said I. 'We're sorry for speaking to you as we did that day on the beach,' he said, 'we realize now that you didn't take our lobsters.' 'Keep your mouth shut,' I said, 'and maybe you'll get more harvesters. . . .' I fished all that day alone. The other men turned up at Two-Waters, and after the field was cut they had a great night with fiddles and dancing till after midnight. I couldn't sleep for the noise of them. Ingi said she was sorry I hadn't gone to the Two-Waters oats. 'We must repay hatred with kindness,' she said. 'Anna was very hurt.'

I never saw such sorry-looking agriculture as the barley-field of Cleft, where we all gathered next morning —a few droopy golden beards like kings that had been long in exile. The field wasn't worth to cut. But we cut it. And Andrew of Cleft thanked us. He said if we were thirsty he had a barrel of sweet water at the end of his house. That was the meanest most miserable man in the world. He thanked us very much indeed for our trouble. He only wished he could reward us better, he said (and we all knew for a fact he had a thousand pounds, the legacy from his uncle in Australia, in the bank at Hamnavoe.) We left his barley lying like a few slaughtered kings in the high field and we went home. His mean-

ness didn't anger me so much as it might have done because I saw that it was my turn next. My oats had heaved
at the sun like a great slow green wave all summer. Now
the sun had blessed it. The whole field lay brazen and
burnished under a blue sweep of sky. And the wind
blessed it continually, sending long murmurs of fulfilment, whispers, secrets, through the thickly congregated
stalks. 'Your field tomorrow, Bill,' they all said. I had
laid in whisky. Ingi had been brewing and baking for a
week (and now her ale for the first time was beginning to
taste good). She had boiled eight cock chickens for the
harvesters.

The sound of rain and wind woke me after midnight.
I could hear the deep gurgle in the throat of the burn.
'Just a shower,' I said to Ingi who had woken also with
the noise of rain on the window and the sough in the
chimney.

But next morning when I went to the door at first light
my cornfield was all squashed and tangled. And the rain
still fell, flattening, rotting, burning, destroying. It
would have been foolishness trying to cut such mush that
day. All the harvesters went out in the storm to save their
lobster creels. And the man of Malthouse said it was his
turn next for the reaper, 'because Bill,' he said, 'has
missed his turn.'

'It will be a fine day tomorrow,' said Ingi.

The rain lasted a full week.

'The plain truth is,' said Jeremiah of Whalerest,
'you're an unlucky crofter. Some crofters are lucky and
some are not. You're a good fisherman, Bill. Stick to the
sea.'

10

I spent the whole morning in the office behind Mr
Sinclair's general merchant shop in Osmundwall. We had

been perhaps a little bit more cordial than the last time we met, but still it was the same as always with Mr Sinclair and me, as if we were closed up together in a hut in the deep Arctic, with no fire in it.

'Well, Bill,' he said, 'if you just sign this paper I think that will be satisfactory to all concerned. I'm a lonely man since Mrs Sinclair died and my chiefest worry now is the happiness of Ingi. You understand that.'

He had proposed before harvest to lend me and Ingi two hundred and fifty pounds at four per cent interest, so that we could finally establish ourselves. In the first instance the loan was to buy more stock and new fishing gear (I had lost all but five of my creels in the October storm).

'Bill,' said Mr Sinclair, 'before you sign that paper I want you to promise me two things. I want you to promise me, for the sake of Ingi, that you won't drink so much. Maybe a small dram on a Saturday night, there's no harm in that, and on a market day, and at New Year of course. And the second thing I want you to promise is this, that you'll go to the services on Sunday. Ingi was brought up in a religious home, and I can tell you this, it hurts her that she has to go to the meeting alone every Sabbath. . .'

I signed the agreement without bothering to answer him. My two particular saints are Robert Burns and Tom Paine. I was not buying two hundred and fifty pounds worth of hypocrisy.

'William,' cried Mr Sinclair sharply. His assistant hurried in from the shop. 'Witness these signatures, William.' William scratched with the pen at the foot of the paper, then went drooping back to the shop.

'I will deposit the money in Ingi's name in the bank at Hamnavoe,' said Mr Sinclair coldly. 'In Ingi's name. Goodbye.'

I cycled back to the valley, fifteen miles.

When I came between the hills I saw a young woman standing in the door of our house, as if she was keeping guard. It was Anna of Two-Waters, a thick strong ugly girl. Jessie of Topmast was at our peatstack, putting peats in her apron.

I leaned the bicycle against the telegraph pole beside the shop. John Wilson the shopkeeper was standing in his door. When he saw me he popped inside like a rabbit. I knew what it was—I was about to become a father, a tainted unlucky outcast until the christening was over.

I leapt across the burn and walked through the wet field towards the house. Across the valley I saw the widow of Girss, a gray shawl on her head. She was moving slowly towards our house.

Anna looked at me with her young freckled wondering face. 'It's Ingi,' she said. My heart failed and faltered and thudded frighteningly at my ribs. 'The house is full of women,' said Anna. 'Her time has come. It isn't easy for her.'

Just then Williamina of Moorfea came to the door, two empty pails in her hand. 'Is she coming?' Williamina said impatiently to Anna. 'Yes,' said Anna, 'I see her now.' 'I'm just going to the burn for water,' said Williamina. Then she turned to me. 'You go away,' she said. 'You're not needed here today. I think you've done enough.'

The widow of Girss was in the next field now.

Jessie of Topmast came round from my peatstack, her apron full of peats. 'Keep away from here,' she said to me sharply. 'You're not wanted.' Her arms were red with attending to my fire.

By now the widow of Girss was at the corner of the house. Two other women came to the door from inside, Elsie of Calvary and Merrag of Sheepay. They received the midwife reverently and speechlessly, as if she was some kind of priestess. 'You clear off,' Elsie of Calvary whispered harshly at me. 'Get down to your boat. Go somewhere out of here.'

The widow of Girss gave me one cold look before she turned in at the door, followed by the other women except Williamina, who was hurrying across the field to the burn, her empty pails clattering.

Inside, Ingi cried out.

I turned away in a panic. First I made for the shore, thought better of it, and turned to the school-house and my old rationalist teacher Mr Simpson. But the gentle murmur of multiplication tables drifted through the tall window and I knew that the school was still in session. I hurried up the hill to my sheep. Andrew of Cleft and John of Sheepay saw me coming and veered away from me, each in a different direction. So did the tinker who had been in the hill all month after rabbits.

I was an outcast in my own valley.

Finally the only man I could find to speak to me was Arthur in the ale-house. I remember little of what he said—for an hour it seemed he reeled off the names of the women who to his knowledge had died in childbirth. But his whisky was a comfort. I stayed at the bar counter till it began to get dark. 'It's a pity,' said Arthur, 'Ingi is not a strong woman.'

The lamp was burning in our window when I crossed the field again. 'To hell with them.' I said, 'It's my own house. I'm going in.' I opened the door softly.

Only the high priestess was inside. The servers had all gone home. She turned to me from the bedside, a gentle sorrowful old woman in the lamplight, the widow of Girss. 'Look', she said. Ingi lay asleep in the bed. A small slow pulse beat in her temple. Her damp hair sprawled all over the pillow; one thin bright strand clung to the corner of her fluttering mouth.

The old woman pointed to the wooden cradle that I
had made in the seven rainy days of harvest.

'There's your son,' said the widow of Girss.

11

Gales of lamentation I could have put up with from the
women, as the terror went through them, the long ritual
keening with which they glutted and purified the world
from the stain of death. (My grandmother and her neighbours went on for three nights before a funeral, their
cries simple and primitive and beautiful as the sea.) Now
minister and elders had told them such exhibitions were
unseemly and godless; the keening had gradually become in the past twenty years a kind of sickly unction, a
litany of the dead person's virtues and sayings and doings
—most of them lies—repeated over and over again, a
welter of sentimental mush.

The black keening I could have endured.

Ingi lay in the bed, long and pale as a quenched candle.
From time to time the child woke up in his cradle and
gave a thin cry. Then Anna of Two-Waters would stir
and attend to him, while the flat litany went on and on.
As for me, I was more of an outcast than ever. None of
them paid the slightest attention to me. Once Anna of
Two-Waters said, 'Do something. Go and feed the kye.
You'll feel better.'

On the third day the missionary came. He opened his
bible and the shallow grief of the women became formal,
austere, beautiful.

> *Or ever the silver cord be loosed, or the golden bowl
> be broken, or the pitcher be broken at the fountain, or
> the wheel broken at the cistern. Then shall the dust
> return to earth as it was: and the spirit shall return
> unto God who gave it.*

We buried Ingi that day. Four of us lowered her into her grave—her father, Howie of Two-Waters, Mr Simpson the teacher, myself.

The missionary stood at the graveside and murmured:

All flesh is grass, and the glory of flesh is as the flower thereof. The grass withereth, the flower fadeth, but the word of the Lord shall endure forever.

Afterwards all the men returned from the kirkyard to the house. The women were still there, silent now. 'Give the men whisky,' I said to the widow of Girss, 'and I'll take a cupful myself.' There were two full bottles and a score of cups on the table.

Anna of Two-Waters sat at the fire with the child in her arms. Ever since Ingi's death Anna had fed him and washed him and comforted him. 'Do you want to die as well?' she said to me. 'You haven't eaten for four days. That whisky will finish you.'

'She's in a happier place, poor Ingi,' said Mr Sinclair among the old women. 'That's true,' they cried in their different voices.

'She's in the earth,' I said. 'We've just done putting her there. The ground isn't a particularly happy place to be.'

'She's by with all her troubles,' said Merrag of Sheepay.

The mourners drank the whisky and one by one shook my hand silently and went off home. The missionary stood beside me, dispensing uneasy unction, but I wouldn't speak to him. Mr Sinclair came over to me and said, 'Peter of Two-Waters has spoken to me. As far as I'm concerned it'll be all right. Anna is a hardworking girl. You should think about it. . . .' I didn't know what the man was talking about, 'You'll get your money all right,' I said. 'Go away.'

Anna of Two-Waters put a bowl of hot soup on the table in front of me. 'Eat that,' she said.

The house was getting emptier all the time, as one by one the women made off homeward, their death watch over. At last there were only three of us left, the missionary, Anna of Two-Waters, myself. I heard Mr Sinclair's car coughing distantly among the Coolags.

'Mr McVey the Osmundwall minister has agreed to christen the child on Wednesday next week,' said the missionary.

'He needn't bother,' I said. 'I'm not having any nonsense of that kind.'

Silently the missionary went away.

The child slept, and Anna of Two-Waters rocked the cradle on the stone floor. It was growing dark.

'My father has spoken to me,' she said, 'and so has Mr Sinclair. Finish your soup now.'

'What were they speaking to you about?' I said.

'Somebody must look after this bairn and this house,' said Anna, 'when you're fishing and ploughing. I don't like *you* at all, but I love this bairn of Ingi's. And so I'll do it.'

'Go away,' I said.

'Maybe I'll get used to you after a time,' said Anna.

'Get away out of here, you ugly bitch,' I shouted at her. I took the sleeping baby from the cradle and carried him outside. The first stars shone on him. I carried him down over the fields to the beach. We stood before a slow darkening heave of sea. A fleck of spindrift drifted on to his cheek. The wind had lain in the south-west since before his birth and Ingi's death. He slept on in my arms, with the bitter blessing of the sea on him.

'Be honest,' I said, 'Be against all darkness. Fight on the side of life. Be against ministers, lairds, shopkeepers. Be brave always.'

When I got home Anna was lighting the lamp.

'Put the bairn back in his cradle,' said Anna, 'and then get to bed yourself. You haven't slept for nights. You're a fool.'

She put on her shawl and moved towards the door.

'I'll be back in the morning,' she said.

12

Anna came through the fields from the Christmas service in the school, carrying the shawled child in her arms. I met her at the burn.

'I do believe,' said Anna, 'you've let the fire go out! There's no smoke from the chimney.'

A cold north wind streamed between the Coolags and the Ward over the valley. The stones rang like iron under our feet. Black bags of cloud bursting with snow sat heavily on the hills.

'Everything's settled,' I said to Anna. 'Peter your father has agreed to take over the croft from me. I'm going to concentrate on the fishing. I'll fish for both families, of course. I'm a lucky fisherman. We're to go on living in the house.'

'Yes,' said Anna, 'I think that's the best plan.'

The child was warm enough. His small face lay against Anna's shoulder with the eyes open and a faint flush on the cheeks.

There were times I could scarcely look into the shifting pool of his face; the skull stared back at me through a thousand trembling resemblances. But today he was a baby like any other baby, a small blind sack of hungers. He began to cry.

'He's tired,' said Anna.

My twenty sheep moved on the hill above the house. In the new year they would belong to old Peter of Two-Waters.

We looked into the byre as we went past. It was warm with the breath of the five kneeling animals. I would have to feed them more hay and turnips before it got darker. The old cow looked round at us with shifting jaws, grave and wondering.

'God help any poor body,' said Anna, 'that has no home on a cold night like this. God help tinkers and all poor wandering folk.'

'Yes,' I said, 'and don't forget the drunkard in the ditch.'

The fire wasn't out after all. There was a deep glow in the heart of the peats. Anna broke the red core with the poker; flames flowered everywhere in the fireplace, and the room was suddenly alive with the rosy shifting dapple.

'It was a beautiful service,' said Anna, 'just lovely. All about Mary and Joseph and the baby and the shepherds and the three kings. I wish you had been there. Who would ever think such things could happen in a byre? Merrag of Sheepay had a new hat on her head. And peedie Tom was so good.'

Before morning, I knew, the valley would be a white blank. And the sea would be flat with the first frost of winter. And, beyond The Kame, fathoms down, the shoals of cod would be moving, bronze soundless streaming legions.

I went out to the shed where I kept my fishing gear.

A Treading of Grapes

THE parish church of St. Peter's stands at one end of a sandy bay on the west coast of Orkney. It is a small square stone utilitarian structure built in the year 1826 by the freely-given labour of all the parishioners; women are said to have carried the stones from the quarry three miles away on their backs, a slow, holy, winter-long procession. But there were churches there before the present church was erected. The inscribed tombs in the churchyard go back to the seventeenth century, and there are older anonymous stones. The minister of St. Peter's in the year 1795 was the Rev. Dr Thomas Fotheringhame. He was the author of two volumes of sermons published in Edinburgh. He complained in a written account of the parish that 'the Kirk roof is full of leakings and dribblings in the winter time, and of draughts at all seasons of the year, whereby the parishioners are like to catch their death of cold, and often my discourses are broken by reason of their hoastings and coughings. The masonry is much delapidated.' . . . It was soon after this that plans were drawn up by the laird for the building of the present church on the same site. But there were other churches there even before Dr Fotheringhame's wet and draughty edifice. Among the clustering tombstones is a piece of a wall with a weathered hole in it that looks as though it might have been an arched window, and slightly to one side an abrupt squat arrangement of dressed stones that suggests an altar. The Rev. Dr Fotheringhame says curtly, 'There is in the vicinity of the Kirk remnants of a popish chapel, where the ignorant yet resort in time of sickness and dearth to leave offerings, in the vain hope that such superstition will alleviate their sufferings; the which Romish embers I have exerted myself to stamp out with all severity during the period of my ministry.' . . . Of this older church nothing is known, except that the priest here at the time of the Reformation was called Master John Halcrow. A fragment of a sermon—for the second Sunday after Epiphany in the year 1548—was recently discovered in a folder of old documents in the laird's cellar. Script and parchment are in the style of the early sixteenth century, and it is possible that Father Halcrow was the preacher.

The source of Father Halcrow's sermon is the gospel account of the wedding feast at Cana in Galilee. Since we also have sermons on the same text by Dr Fotheringhame (August 1788) and by the present incumbent, Rev. Garry Watters, B.D. (Edin.)—the latter sermon preached earlier this year and reproduced by courtesy of the editor of the parish magazine—it might be of interest, as showing the changing style of the Scottish sermon through the centuries, to set them out, one after the other, beginning with that of Mr Watters.

*　　*　　*

(1)

Rev. Garry Watters

'I wonder what you were thinking of, when you listened to this New Testament lesson? I'm sure some of you were thinking of the last wedding you were at, perhaps a month ago, or a year ago, or even ten years ago. You were thinking, of course, of the church, and the young couple standing there together in the empty choir, and the minister in solemn tones performing the marriage ceremony. Yes, but I suppose that you were thinking particularly of the reception afterwards in the hotel, for this piece of scripture, strangely enough, has nothing to say about the marriage ceremony at all; it's all about the reception. I'm sure you're seeing again in your mind's eye all the cars standing in the hotel car park, and the long tables covered with flowers and food, and guests being introduced to one another, and then—a crowning moment—when the happy young couple entered to take their places, with confetti in the bride's veil and on the shoulders of the bridegroom's new suit. Then the meal, to the accompaniment of lighthearted conversation, and the toasts and the speeches—some wittier than others, I suppose—and the reading of the many telegrams, and the furtive moment when the young newly-weds slip away to their secret honeymoon destination. Perhaps there will have been a talented singer or two among the guests. Certainly there was music and dancing. This never-to-be-forgotten day ended with the singing of Auld Lang Syne.

'Yes, you remember it all vividly. What you will have forgotten, in the sheer enjoyment of it all, is how smoothly everything happened. Everything went to schedule. But—and now I'm coming to the important thing—you would certainly have remembered this wedding, with some pain and embarrasment, if, for example, the organist had played Wagner instead of Mendelssohn for the entry of the bride, or if the wedding cake had not been delivered from the baker's in time, or if the toast order had got all mixed up, or if the taximen had driven the bride's parents to the wrong hotel.

'Now this is exactly what happened in the gospel story—somebody blundered. The refreshments ran done. The whole wedding reception was threatened with disaster. A thing like that is remembered for a long time in a small place. In the little town of Cana they would have gossiped about this badly-organized wedding for many a day, would they not?

'Fortunately, Jesus was a guest at the wedding, and he very quickly put things to right, at once, no nonsense about it; smoothly and efficiently he took over, and everything was straightened out. Not only that, but the wedding went with a greater swing than before.

'We read about miracles, but—ask yourselves this—what exactly is a miracle? It is not some kind of superior conjuring trick—it is rather, I'm inclined to think myself, the exercise of a supreme common sense, a looking at every conceivable eventuality with absolute clear-sightedness and understanding, so that the remedy is clear even before the difficulty arises. Turning water into wine is merely a graphic shorthand for the way in which the foresight of Jesus more than compensated for the steward's blundering. He made sure beforehand that the neglected supplies were to hand.

'He is the best organiser, the best planner who ever lived. You may be sure we can trust him with our smallest everyday affairs. He won't ever let us down.

'Think, in the wider sphere, what a brilliant business executive, what a wise ambassador, what a competent minister of state he would have made! In his hands we can safely leave the troubles and frictions that distract the world we live in. Amen.

'There's just one thing I must mention before the final hymn. Up to now, in this church, on the four occasions each year that we celebrate the Sacrament of the Lord's Supper, a wine has been used that contained a certain small percentage of alcohol. Of recent years there has been, in this congregation and indeed all over Scotland, a large and growing demand for unfermented wine to be used in the sacrament, as being more seemly. Consequently, next Sunday, after the morning service, a ballot will be taken of all the members of the congregation present, as to whether you want fermented wine at future sacraments, or an unfermented substitute more in keeping, it may be, with the seemliness of our devotions.'

(2)

Dr Thomas Fortheringhame

'Brethren, some of you might be thinking that the piece of gospel I read out just this minute anent the Lord Christ's turning of water into wine at Cana of Galilee is divine permission to you to make drunken beasts of yourselves at every wedding that takes place within the bounds of this parish this coming winter; ay, and not only at every wedding but at every christening forby and every funeral and harvest supper. It is the devil of hell that has put such a thought into your minds. It never says in holy writ that any wedding guest was drunk at Cana of Galilee.

'Magnus Learmonth, you in the second pew from the back, at the wedding you made for your third lass Deborah at Skolness at the back end of Lammas, all the guests lay at the ale-kirn like piglets about the teats of a sow till morning, to the neglect even of dancing; and two women in this same district came to themselves next morning in the ditch of Graygyres. Bella Simison, you do well to hang your head there at the back of the Kirk— it argues a small peck of grace. Andrina of Breck, you were the other defaulter—don't look at me like that, woman!—you have a brazen outstaring impudence commensurate with your debauchery. Well I know you and your runnings back and fore between Breck and the ale-house with your bit flask under your shawl. Things are told privily into my lug.

'What this text argues, brethren, is that the host at the

wedding, the bridegroom's good-father, was a careful and a prudent man with his bawbees. No doubt this provident man said to himself the day the marriage bids were sent about the countryside with a hired horseman, "If I order too few pigs of drink, they'll say I keep the pursestrings drawn over tight, and if I order too muckle they'll say I'm a spendthrift. And so I find myself between devil and deep. What is the right quantity of drink for a celebration such as this?" . . . Being a prudent man, I say, he ordered too few pigs of drink (only it wasn't pigs of usquebaugh, whisky, in that foreign place, nor yet ale; it was jars of wine). The which when the Lord came he corrected, he set to right, as he will beyond a doubt set to right all our exaggerations and our deficiencies, since only he kens what is stinted and what is overblown in the nature of every man born. He adds and he takes from. The stringent economy of the host drew no rebuke from him. He accomplished the miracle. Then there was dancing, then there was fiddling, then no doubt near midnight bride and groom were carried into the ben room with roughness and sly jokes and a fiddle and five lanterns.

'Nor was this the end of meat and drink as far as the Lord was concerned. You ken all about the multiplication of the five bannocks and the two cod-fish, concerning which I preached to you for an hour and more last Sabbath. There came a night at the supper-board when he suddenly took an oat-cake and broke it and raised his jug of drink and leaned across and said to them who were no doubt wanting to fill their bellies without any palaver, "This is my body," he said, and then, "This is my blood" – a most strange and mystifying comparison indeed, that the papists would have us believe to be a literal and real and wholly breath-taking change of substance effected by a form of words. Whatever it means, brethren – and our General Assembly has not and doubtless will not

bind you to any infallible conclusions as to the signifi-
cance of these utterances—whatever it means, it teaches
us a terrible reverence for the things we put in our mouths
to nourish us, whether it is the laird's grouse and claret or
the limpets that Sam of the Shore eats with cold water out
of the well in the lean days of March.

'You will not go home, therefore, and hog down your
brose like swine in a sty or like cuddies at a trough. The
common things you put in your mouths are holy mysteries indeed, beyond the taste and the texture. Therefore,
brethren, with reverence you will make them a part of
your body and your life.

'Prudence, my brethren, a proper proportioning of our
goods, estimation, forethought—so much to the King, so
much to the laird, so much to the Kirk, so much for the
maintainance of ourselves and them that belong to us, so
much to the poor—that is doubtless the meaning of this
text; and for the things we lack, that we should ask the
Lord to supply them, and so rest content in our estate.

'John Sweynson, I observe that you bought a new
shawl to your wife's head at the Kirkwall Market, with
what looks to be silken lacing round the edge of it, a
thing of vanity, and new black lace gloves to her hands.
She will not darken this kirk door again, no nor you either,
with these Babylonish things on her body.

'Samuel Firth, of the operations of your farm, Dale in
the district of Kirkbister, naturally I ken nothing, nor
does it concern me. But you have seven black cows on the
hill if you have one, and fifty sheep forby, and a hundred
geese. Is it a proper and a godly thing, think you, that
your three small bairns sit in the front pew there under
the precentor blue and channering with the cold, they
having no right sarks to their backs nor boots to their
feet? Have a care of this, look to it, as you call yourself a
Christian. Amen.

'Concluding, I have two announcements to make. John Omand, on account of the bastard child he fathered on Maria Riddoch at Michelmas, appeared before the Kirk session on Wednesday and being duly constrained answered *Yea* to the accusation, wherefore he will suffer public rebuke three sequent Sabbaths in this Kirk on the stool of penitence, beginning next Sabbath.

'I hear that the French brig *Merle*, Monsieur Claude Devereux, master, discharged some cargo at the Bay of Ostray in the darkness of Friday night. The gentlemen of the excise were at Kirkwall, playing at cartes. Will you, therefore, James Drever, deliver as usual a keg of best brandy at the Manse tomorrow morning, when Mistress Skea my serving woman will see that you are recompensed for your pains.'

(3)

FATHER HALCROW

The   'Cometh the full grape cluster upon the vine. The
Vine   rain falleth. Clusters thicken, purple they are as bruises, as thunder, yet each grape containeth within itself a measure of joy and dancing, the quick merry blood of the earth.

Grape   'Cometh at last the hour of full ripeness.
Harvest   Labourers toil all day, they cram the baskets, their arms are red. The master of the vineyard, he goeth about the streets in the last of the sun, bargaining with such as sit idle against the wall and them that throw dice in the dust. For the grape harvest must be ingathered.

The Treading   'And he that presseth the hoarded grapes,
of Grapes   look, his breast and his thighs are red, as though he had endured a terrible battle, himself scathe-

less. And still more and more grapes are brought to the press where he laboureth, this hero.

Wine 'Now it standeth long, the vat, in a cellar under earth, as it were in a cold grave. Yet this is in no wise a station of death. Put thy ear against the vat, thou hearest a ceaseless murmur, a slow full suspiration. The juice is clothing itself in sound, in song, in psalmody.

The Wine 'Now see the vinter in his shop, bottles,
 Shop barrels, wineskins all about him. There cometh a steward that is preparing a wedding, a feast of note, his master's daughter will be married. This feast is not to be any mouse-in-the-cupboard affair, no, it will be a costly ceremony with harps and tapestries and bits of silver thrown to the children in the street outside. What does the vinter think—will seven jars of wine be enough? Or twelve? Or three? It is hard to say how much the guests will drink. Many strangers are bidden. They might sip with small burgess mouths or they might have throats like salt mines. He cannot tell.

The Six 'In the end they agreed together upon so many
 Jars jars of wine, six let us say, after much calculation according to the wisdom of this world.

The 'Under the first star they travel, the wedding
Guests guests, such a crowd as you would see on any Orkney feast day—ploughman and mason and laird and labourer and grieve and notary and beachcomber, and a horde of women, besides one or two persons unbidden—in holy-day coats they crowd to one house with lights and music in it. There they will celebrate the sacrificial feast of a maidenhead.

The 'And presently in the door stands the carpenter
Word of Nazareth, and his mother and twelve more

forby that have a smell of fish and seaweed and limpets on them from their trade, all known faces. Yet none guessed that here was The Incarnate Word (had they not bargained with him for cradles and chairs and roof-beams?). None knew that here was Mary, Queen of Angels, Mystical Rose, Gate of Heaven, Holy Mother of God (had she not washed her linen a many a time with the other women at the burn?).

Rose of 'A bell strikes silence upon their babble. From
Love this door and that door bridegroom and bride issue, separately they come forth. They stand together at last. They wait for all their random lusts, longings, desires, burnings to be gathered up into the one rose of human love. Cometh a priest and blesseth them. Then all the harps break out in one concert of joy.

The Empty 'The steward maketh a sign. Now is the
Jars time for all those guests—rich and poor, young and old, farmer and fisherman, widow and maiden, to mingle together—so that this chamber seemeth to be in little the whole world and its tumultuous folk. The first jar is emptied into a hundred cups. The bridegroom, where is he? Secretly twelve handmaidens light lamps. The bridegroom has gone into his chamber. The handmaidens carry the bride through a door. The harps play. The steward is busy between the music and the wine. The cups go round and round. A handful of silver sklinters like rain among the children in the dark close outside. Sand runs in the hourglass, candles dwindle, the night passeth. And then one cometh, a serving man, and saith to the steward *The wine is all finished* while as yet the first flush is not upon the faces of musicians and dancers.

The 'Consider what a common thing is water. We
Water set small value upon it except when the well is

nothing but a few burning stones. When there is abundance of water we turn up the collars of our coats and we curse the rain. I tell you the guests at that marriage feast in Cana thought but poorly of it when the empty wine jars were filled to the brim with water at the behest of this carpenter from Nazareth. And the steward was distraught and the host's brow dark with vexation; he was like to be held in disgrace a many a day for his improvidence. And yet the woman reassureth the entire company, *Quodcumque dixerit vobis, facite* – 'Do whatsoever he telleth you to do.' So sweetly she urgeth that the serving men run to obey. Now the as-yet-unmiracled Word standeth among the water jars.

The 'The souls and creatures of that house – in *Miracle* particular the element of water – become utterly subject unto The Word, as all creation was in the six days of its becoming. The devious stations by which water becometh wine – the tap-root, grafting, pruning, sun, blossoming, wind, fruition, harvest, press, leaven, vat, vintry – all that long vexation was here cancelled. The Word spanned all creation, as it did in the paradise of Eden before Adam delved and Eve span. And a serving man poureth a jar of this new water. At once their cups brim with red circles. The trembling lips of the steward approve the mystery. Then all their mouths break out in celebration, like angels and holy souls that praise God forever with their *Sanctus* and their *Gloria*.

* * *

'Dear children, this I have spoken of is a most famous marriage. We are poor people, fisherman and crofters, and we think it is not likely in these the days of our vanity that we will be bidden to such a feast. We are poor people, Olaf the fisherman and Jock the crofter and Merran the hen-wife, we are pleased enough with oatcakes and ale at

our weddings, we were born to hunger and meikle hard-
ship, and there will be a single candle burning beside us
the night they come to straik us and to shroud us.

'No, but this is not true. Let me tell you a secret.
Christ the King, he hath uplifted our fallen nature as
miraculously as he clothed water in the red merry robes
of wine. Very rich and powerful you are, princes, poten-
tates, heirs and viceroys of a Kingdom. So opulent and
puissant are you, dear ones, for that each one of you has
in his keeping an immortal soul, a rich jewel indeed, more
precious than all the world beside. So then, princes (for
I will call you Olaf the fisherman and Jock the crofter no
longer but I will call you by the name the Creator will
call you in the last day) princes, I say, I have good news
for you, you are bidden every one to a wedding. Get
ready your gifts, get ready your shoes to the journey.
What wedding? you ask, *we know of no wedding.* I answer,
*The marriage of Christ with His Church. And where will this
marriage be?* you ask. *Everywhere*, I answer, *but in particular, lords and princes, in this small kirk beside the sea
where you sit. And when is it to be, this wedding?* you ask
me. *Always*, I answer, *but in particular within this hour,
now, at the very moment when I bow over this bread of your
offering, the food, princes and lords, that you have won with
such hard toil from the furrows, at once when I utter upon it
five words* HIC EST ENIM CORPUS MEUM. Then is
Christ the King come once again to his people, as truly
as he was present at the marriage in Cana, and the Church
his bride abides his coming, and this altar with the few
hosts on it and the cup is a rich repast indeed, a mingling
of the treasures of earth and heaven, and the joy of them
in Cana is nothing to the continual merriment of the
children of God. *Sanctus sanctus sanctus*, they cry forever
and ever, *Benedictus qui venit in nomine Domini*.

'Dance ye then, princes and ladies, in your homespun,

there is no end to this marriage, it goes on at every altar of the world, world without end. This Bread that I will raise above your kneeling, It is entire Christ—Annunciation, Nativity, Transfiguration, Passion, Death, Resurrection, Ascension, Majesty, gathered up into one perfect offering, the Divine Love itself, whereof you are witnesses.

'And not only you, princes, all creation rejoices in the marriage of Christ and His Church, animals, fish, plants, yea, the water, the wind, the earth, the fire, stars, the very smallest grains of dust that blow about your cornfields and your Kirkyards.'

In Nomine Patris et Filii et Spiritus Sancti. Amen.

*   *   *

I walked along the road past St. Peter's church this morning.

On the beach a few fishing boats were hauled out of reach of the waves. Behind the church lay the farms and crofts of the parish, tilth and pasture, the mill, the school, the smithy, the shop. In the field next the church a tractor moved jerkily, trailing an airy drove of gulls; it is the time of ploughing. The young man in the tractor seat suddenly stood up and shouted, he swung his arm in wide circles. A girl throwing oats to a white agitation of hens at the end of a byre two fields away acknowledged his summons with a mere movement of her hand, a suggestion of greeting. Then she went quickly indoors (so that the neighbours wouldn't be getting any ideas for gossip). But the January air, I thought, was sweeter for that small promise of replenishment; and perhaps Mr Watters will soon have another wedding sermon to preach.

The sea shattered and shattered on the beach.

The wind from the sea soughed under the eaves of the Kirk, and among tombstones with texts and names newly

chiselled on them, and those with withered half-obliter-
ated lettering, and those that have lost their meanings
and secrets to very ancient rain.

Icarus

THERE are some folk who take a great delight in prophesying the end of the world. It is a kind of hobby with them. They sit around with pencils and bits of paper, and they work out, by manipulating some of the obscure symbols and figures in Revelation, the very day and hour when doom will fall. They've never brought it off yet, but they keep on trying.

My Uncle Tom is one of those people. 'Old Apocalypse' they call him in the smithy. So it was no surprise to me when two Sundays ago, he whispered in my ear: 'Thursday, ten past two in the afternoon.' We had spent a very pleasant evening round the fire, talking about shipwrecks and tinkers and storms. Aunt Bella's ale had been in splendid condition. Finally, towards midnight, I had risen to go home, and suddenly all the laughter went out of Tom and he said: 'Thursday, ten past two in the afternoon.' Bella clucked disapprovingly in the background. She doesn't hold with all that nonsense.

No more do I, and I forgot all about it till the Wednesday evening, when I called along at their croft with a few haddocks I had caught off Hoy that afternoon. Bella herded me into the straw chair beside the fire and put a bowl of ale in my hands. While she gutted the fish she told me, in one riotous spate of gossip, what couples were getting married and what girls were having babies and what boys had got summonses for running their bikes without a licence.

'Where's Tom?' I said.

The last haddock tail went flying from her scissors.

'He's out in the shed,' she said sharply, 'making ready for Thursday.'

I wandered out to the shed. I didn't go in, for when the prophetic mood is on my Uncle Tom he's no fun at all. I looked through the window, and there he was working on the weirdest contraption that ever was. The bench was piled with a complication of wood and canvas and leather straps and Tom was hammering away at it furiously. I never saw anything quite like it.

I went back into the kitchen to finish my ale.

'What's he making?' I asked Bella.

'Wings,' she said. 'The old fool.'

Then she got on to talking about her favourite subjects – Jo Grimond and the local strathspey society. She was a lot more cheerful by the time I left.

The next day, Thursday, was the Dounby Show. If you've never been to the Dounby Show you've missed one of the wonders of the north. All the nine parishes meet together that day in two small fields beside the village. All the beauty and splendour of their live-stock are on show – proud ponderous Clydesdales, bulls like black cubes (oh, the majesty and stupidity of their curled brows!), sheep with mild snowy fleeces, caged cockerels giving the sun a raging salute every five minutes. Among them wander the laird with his deerstalker and shooting-stick, and Sam the tinker, and everyone in between. Besides, the showmen from the south are there, with their shooting stalls and swingboats and coconut shies. The one little pub in the village is crammed to the doors, and the overflow congregate in the huge gloom of the marquee.

I was having my fortune told by a draped woman who called herself 'Madame Roberta, the World's Greatest Palmist', when it suddenly struck me that this was the afternoon that the world was to end.

Today, at ten past two, *Finis* was to be scrawled in brim-
stone under the long rambling incoherent tragic comic
fiction of man's life on earth. I looked at my watch. The
time was half-past two.

Uncle Tom was wrong again.

'And I see that you've had one or two wee disappoint-
ments', went on Madame Roberta in her Aberdeen accent.
'But you've got over them. You're going to have a good
harvest. That last cow you bought is going to have *three*
calves.'

I didn't have the heart to tell her I was a fisherman.

Madame Roberta's voice sank to a whispered chant.
'I see a girl,' she said, 'a tall beautiful girl with fair hair.
Give me another two bob and I'll tell you all about her.
. . .'

The prophets are not doing so well today, I thought,
as I emerged from the fortune-telling booth into the full
glare and blare of the show. But Madame Roberta is less
wrong than Old Apocalypse down there beside the loch.

For life goes on.

That evening, when inn and marquee closed and the
last drunkard went home under the moon, I cycled to the
croft to see how Uncle Tom was taking his latest dis-
appointment.

The first thing I saw when I turned in at the gate was
the contraption, the wing machine. It was lying on the
grass like a strange discarded chrysalis.

Aunt Bella was knitting beside the fire.

'What like was the show?' she said.

'Splendid,' I said. 'That best I ever saw.'

Actually it was a pretty ordinary show but when I have
the tang of ale on my palate I tend to exaggerate.

'Where's Tom?' I said.

'The ambulance took him away to the hospital an hour
ago,' she said mildly. 'He broke his leg.'

And then, while a gray sock grew out of her clicking needles and her spectacles glinted in the firelight, she unfolded the story. The wings, of course, had been for Tom to fly into the sky. It had taken Bella most of the morning to get him harnessed. Then, during dinner (the last meal anybody would ever eat on this earth, he assured her), Tom had decided that he would get a better take-off from the roof. It had taken a great deal of pushing and shoving to get him on to the thatch. The neighbours had come out to see the spectacle, and that had made Bella 'black affronted'. It was all right when he used to sit quietly in the ben room waiting for the trump to blow.

The minutes ticked away. Tom kept looking at his watch. People going to the Show stopped to gape at this free spectacle. A trout fisher on the loch looked up with suspended oars. A seagull lighted for a moment on the canvas tip of Tom's right wing. There was complete silence for a few minutes on the hillside.

'Are you down there, Bella?' said Tom at last.

'Yes,' she said, 'I'm here.'

'Would you go in and see what time it is on the alarm clock? My watch says *twelve* minutes past two. . . .' Bella could have sworn he was crying just then.

She came out again and said: 'It's fourteen and a half minutes past two.'

Thereupon Tom had his moment of splendid rebellion. He stood erect on the thatch and spread his wings. Then he gave a loud cry and launched himself on the afternoon; and, a presumptuous Icarus, fell beside the peat stack in a wild disorder of legs and canvas and outraged fluttering hens.

Bella left him lying where he was and went across the road to phone for the doctor.

*　　　*　　　*

ICARUS

I visited Uncle Tom in hospital last Sunday. He was very cheerful. He spoke about past Dounby Shows and about a darkie who had once come there when he was a boy. This darkie had lain down naked on a bed of nails with three ploughmen standing on him. Afterwards he had licked a red-hot poker, and said 'Sugar!' rolling his eyes round the crowd.

I spent a very pleasant hour with him. Only when I was leaving I noticed, on top of his locker, a small bible open at Revelation, and a piece of paper with calculations scrawled all over it.

'You're still at it,' I said.

'Nineteen sixty-five,' he said, 'June the twenty-fourth. Only I can't make out yet whether it'll be five past four in the morning or ten to eight at night.'

Apart from that, he's getting along as well as can be expected.

The Story Teller

'No,' they said to the old man in the Hamnavoe Bar, 'a story about women.'

There were two crofters, Thorfinn Vik and Ronald Leask, standing at the bar, and Jock Henryson the fisherman. Drew the barman was laughing at a story that had just finished, and slapping his thigh. Two draught players sat in the dark corner, enchanted over the board.

It was about half past eight on a Friday evening.

'What women?' said the old man. He was half way through his second pint of heavy beer. 'The less said about women the better.' He thought for a minute, then he said, 'Here is my story of The Two Women, a love story. Listen.'

1

My father said to me after the harvest, 'Now your mother's a ruckle of bones in the kirkyard, there's nobody to knit sea stockings for us. There's nobody to put cheese and ale in our pockets when we go out to plough. There's nobody to have a fire burning when we come back from the fishing.'

'That's true,' I said.

Then he mentioned a name, Katie of Moorfea.

'What are you saying that name for?' I said. 'Why are you always mentioning that widow? Why do you say the name of a hag like that night and morning in my ear?'

'She's to be your wife,' said he. 'I won't argue about it. You'll go and see her tonight.'

My father was a masterful terrible man. Never once in my life had I crossed him. I knew the way his mind was working, apart from the sea stockings, the cheese and ale, and the fire in the hearth. Our boat *Solveig* was old; he could buy a new yawl with the dowry.

I went to see Katie of Moorfea in the darkening of that same day. You would hear the screeches of her across the valley most days. But this sunset, as I stood in the door of Moorfea, her syllables were gentle as a dove. But her face was as red and cloven and harsh as The Sneuk, that crag out in the bay.

'Come in,' she said sweetly. In I went after her.

The girl Sara was sitting at the fire. She looked at me and then at her mother, and then she rose up with her knitting needles and wool, and into the ben room with her, leaving a small sweet scent in the air. Why had I never noticed that before? I had been seeing her every day for seventeen years. I had sat beside her in the school and never got one whiff of that enchantment.

The bud lives in its own tightness. Then one morning the rose opens, and the air around it is all exciting and rich.

Says old Katie, 'Your father spoke to me. I will take you. I'm forty comes September but an active woman at board and in bed. I have twenty-four pounds ten shillings in a stocking under the bed. . . .' Then down with her like an old bitch on all fours to find the loaded stocking under the bed that was to shackle me to her forever. She pawed and growled there in the darkness like a mongrel digging for rabbits. Then says she after a while in a shrouded voice, 'I'm stuck, man, pull me out.'

Her backside was wedged there like a great cheese in a press. I put my foot against it and I jammed her in under the bed tighter, and says I, 'Keep your dowry. Better you under the bed than on top!'

And I fixed my cap on my head with a flourish and ben I went into the next room. Katie began to howl like an animal in a trap. I was eager to find Sara in the dark. 'Sara,' I whispered. There she was right enough, a tall sweet trembling shape. 'What's wrong with my mother?' she said. 'She's guarding her treasure,' says I, 'like some old dragon.' I leaned forward to find her mouth. There was a quick blinding pain across my face. Drops of blood spattered on the back of my hand like heavy red warm coins. I looked down and saw two knitting needles growing out of my groin, quivering.

I lay in bed for a week afterwards.

The scars of Sara's nails are in my face to this day. Further down are two red gnarls that I will take to the grave with me.

In the end I married neither of these women. My father never spoke a word to me all that winter. He would glare and glamp every time I came in through the door. I would catch him glowering at me over the nets. The *Solveig* warped slowly, and day by day let in more sea water. My days gathered and fell like drops of vinegar. Also there was some blood still from my wounds, a slow seeping; Sara's needles had woven drawers of fire for me that kept me in torment a full winter.

At the end of January Sara married a farmer from Brims, a black twisted stick of a man. You've seen a rose growing in the heart of a thorn.

It was a hard winter for me.

In March I joined the *Pearl*, a whaling ship, here in Hamnavoe. I was away all summer till after harvest, among the icebergs and the whales, an iron spear in my fist by day, and by night a pack of gambling cards or a rum bottle, and once or twice a knife when it came to fighting.

When I got back to Orkney, in October, I found the old man sitting in the door making lobster creels. There was a new boat in the noust, a cluster of beautiful white curves and as fine a cleave of bow as ever I saw. My father let on not to be surprised to see me, as if I had been away at the shop on the other side of the hill for a plug of tobacco, maybe, or a ball of twine.

'I see we have a new boat,' I said.

'*I* have a new boat,' he said. 'Myself and my wife have a new boat. And thanks be, she's landed some good catches this summer, that same boat.'

I saw the name *Katie* painted on her bow.

'Come in, Andrew, your broth's ready,' a voice from inside the house screamed out.

'Yes,' said my father meekly, 'I'm coming.' Then into his own house he went, that terrible old man, smirking and cringing.

Then I knew for sure I had a new mother that wouldn't be good to me.

I never married to this day.

I began to build my own house that same afternoon. I gathered red stones from the beach under Rora Head.

That's my story of The Two Women.

* * *

'That story about the sea now,' said Drew the barman. He breathed into a whisky glass and rubbed it bright with his apron.

'There's a thousand stories about the sea,' said the old man, 'bad ones mostly. Better to keep quiet about the

sea . . .!' He drank a good mouthful out of his fourth pint.
'The less said about the sea the better.'

The men went on speaking about other things, the
Longhope Regatta on Friday and the Dounby Market the
Thursday after that.

The barman said, 'You know, the *Greatheart*.'

The drinking and the random talk went on. The
draught players bent over the draught-board, silent enchanted men. Everyone let on to ignore the old man.

'Here is my story of The Fishing Boat,' he said at last.
'Listen.'

2

It was a blue bright windy morning, I mind. You know
the way a knife gets whetted on a gray stone, till it
glitters like new. That's the way the sun lay on the sea,
turning and gleaming and whetting itself.

Amos and I went down to the beach after our breakfast.
We pushed the *Greatheart* out. 'Glory to God,' said
Amos. Five other boats were out too, *Trust, Margaret,
Siloam, Sadie, Queen.*

We said we would go to the haddocks first. Then we
would haul the lobsters under the cliff as we came back.

I never saw such a shining morning. 'It's like as if the
sea was full of heavenly blessings,' said Amos. 'That's
the way the wings of the angels will be.'

I was often tired of the holy talk of Amos, and yet he was
a good fisherman, and we agreed well enough about
most things.

Five miles west we rowed, till the island of Hoy was a
distant red rampart fronting the Atlantic. We began
to set our lines. 'Open,' said Amos to the sea, 'open
your everlasting doors.' 'For God's sake,' I said,

'shut up and fish.' We commenced to fish. We got a basket of haddocks and some codling and a dog-fish or two. The *Trust* and the *Margaret* were fishing half-a-mile north of us.

There was a block of fog in the west, and a quick flurry or two on the sea, like long invisible coats lightly brushing it and hurrying on, a dark scurry and whisper and rush of unseen feet over the waters.

Amos sang his bits of psalms and hauled in the lines with his thick hairy arms. Every hook burgeoned with sea fruit. 'Hallelujah', said Amos. We got another half basket full.

Then the sun went out like a lamp being snuffed. It was suddenly as eerie as twilight. I looked round and saw the weather coming at us from the north-west. The sea fell on the boat like a breaking wall. I took the knife out of my belt and cut the line. Amos had no knife; he snapped another line with his great square teeth. Then we reeled against one another like drunk fighters. 'May the Lord be—' shouted Amos, but the wind killed the prayer in his throat. *Greatheart* went raging down and sideways like a mad beast among the troughs. I threw myself at the tiller and hung on. Spindrift—swarm after swarm of gray bees—went over the boat, and Amos staggered among them, a gray bee-keeper. He took his brass watch out of his waist-coat pocket, looked at it, and held it up for me to see: why, I don't know, unless it was to mark the hour of his glorification. The watch said twenty minutes to noon—more than an hour till the turn of the tide. I nodded. It was no use speaking in all that tumult about us.

There was no sign of the *Trust* and the *Margaret*.

When we were flung out of the troughs I could see Hoy,

the sun on the crags bright and remote as a dream. Then again the waves were all about us.

The sea wrenched at the rudder till my wrist was nearly broken. I leaned against the thwart to get leverage. The rudder tugged against me like a young bull at the end of a rope. I seized it again and hung on.

'Lord have mercy', was the shape Amos's mouth was making. . . .

There was the black wave and the gray wave and the white wave. Sometimes separately they rose against us, sometimes all three together stood about the boat, sometimes there would be two, the gray wave behind and the black wave before, or the black wave to one side of us and the white wave at the other, an endless reel and onset.

I crouched at the stern. I held the groaning tiller against my chest till my ribs cracked. My ears and nostrils were choked with salt. Continuous spindrift slashed across my face. My vision was broken--I saw the storm through a thousand salt splintering rainbows.

The black wave.

I looked once at Amos, He was kneeling in the middle of the boat, bailing as hard as he could. His mouth was open, laughing. 'That's your holy men for you,' I thought bitterly.

I thought of my sins. I thought of the three pounds of tobacco I got from the French skipper at Longhope and never paid for. There was the eggs I found in Girss's cornfield and put secretly in my pocket. I winked one Sabbath in the Kirk at Jessie of Calvary from behind a hymn-book. I put a stone through the factor's window one night between Yule and Hogmanay, the year he drove the Rackwick men's sheep off

the hill. Lord, I was at the plundering of the Rotter-
dam ship when we threw a Dutch seaman back into the
sea who was not yet dead.

The gray wave.

Lord have mercy on us. Even if the *Greatheart* was driven
against Hoy what kind of a landfall would that be?
The west of Hoy was a line of high red crags, The
Kame, St. John's, The Berry, The Too, The Sneuk,
Santoo, The Kist. Dark terrible angels, they gathered
souls to themselves every winter.

The white wave.

I looked at Amos again and saw a splash of seaweed on
the back of his hand. Why did it not wash off in all the
sea that was lashing in? The red sea-ware moved and
dribbled, but stayed on Amos's labouring hand. It
was a wound. He had cut himself on the sharp edge of
the bailing pan, or on a hook, or on the bone of a cod.
He laughed soundlessly in all that smother, rising and
stooping with the bailing pan, emptying the sea back
into the sea.

The black wave and the white wave.

Yes, and what widows would stand on the shore at Rackwick this night and every night till all the bodies were
found? Bella of The Harp and Jess of Topmast and
Margaret-Ann of Sheepay and Willa of Two-Waters
and Mary of Hawkfall and Sara of Malthouse and
Amos's Rachel with the unborn child in her, dark
shrouded figures among the round red rocks of the
beach. Night would come down from the hills on them,
still their eyes would stare at this moving thing and
that small glimmer out in the bay, bits of driftwood
only, fleeting phosphorescence. They would shake
their heads to one another. Then it would be too dark

to know sea from land. They would walk home separately across the steep fields. Then in the lamplight an unfolding of shrouds, an opening of black bibles, a stony intentness of grief.

For me, nothing. I lit my own lamps. I was beholden to no woman.

The gray wave, the white wave, the black wave.

For me, no-one.

The yellow wave.

Sunlight steepled and shimmered round us from sudden rents in the sky. The bailing pan glittered in Amos's hand. The *Greatheart* stopped lurching. The Sneuk and The Too stood on each side of us like guardians. The white beach was in front of us, the bright bay all around, dancing waters.

Seven yellow waves rolled us on to the Rackwick sand.

Amos took his brass watch in his bleeding hand and we looked at it.

It was ten minutes after noon. The storm had lasted exactly half-an-hour. Rachel with her round sweet belly was on the shore, waving to us.

The *Trust*, the *Margaret*, the *Queen* were broken against the Kame that day. At sunset we knew for sure there were five new widows in the valley.

Amos and I hauled the *Greatheart* up and divided our catch. Rachel buried her small face in Amos's fierce black Habbakuk beard.

I went home then and boiled a cod for my dinner. I was beholden to no woman. I dried my shirt at my own fire.

*　　　*　　　*

Drew put six full pewter mugs on the counter. 'Drink up,' he said. 'That's the last. No more after that.' The clock above the bottles stood at five to ten.

The draught players set up their pieces again on the board.

Ronald Leask of Clett said to the old man, 'One more story.'

'No,' the old man said, 'I'm too dry.'

'Give him a pint,' said Jock Henryson to the barman.

'He's an anointed liar,' said Thorfinn Vik of Helliar on the old man's deaf side. 'He's the biggest liar in Orkney.'

'I am not drunk,' said the old man with dignity. 'But I'm very dry.'

A full pint mug was set at his elbow.

'Here is my story of The Fiddler,' he said. 'Listen.'

'Make it quick,' said the barman.

3

Samuel of Marsh was the kind of fiddler that would take dances out of a cripple man. But quite apart from that it was a very *useful* instrument, his fiddle. Yes, it was more useful than any plough that ever went through a glebe or any net that sieved the sea.

For example, Amos's red cow was in stuck screaming labour and they poured medicines down her and they groped in her heaving umbles, but still her screaming went on for three hours. Samuel came to the byre door with his fiddle. He asked them were they torturing the beast over a slow fire. Then he played a stave or two, and a little white bull calf fell on the straw, as if time had sent a sweet cold summons into the red eternal chaos.

I swear to God Samuel was a beautiful fiddler.

Bill of Sheepay got stones from the beach to build a new barn. From the start everything went wrong. First the weather was bad. Then the Osmundwall mason sent the two laziest brutes of apprentices that God ever put breath in. They sat on their backsides in the byre most of the time smoking and playing cards. If the sun shone they might come out and stoop among the stones, occasionally shifting one. Then it would rain again and back they went to their pipes and their rummy.

At the end of a week the gable was only three feet high.

On the Sunday night Bill of Sheepay went down to Marsh and laid a shilling on Samuel's table. Samuel nodded. Early on the Monday morning Samuel came to Sheepay with his fiddle. He played for an hour. It was a worse day than ever, thunder and rain—you would swear the sky was trundling with a thousand leaky water barrels. But tobacco and knaves-and-aces were forgotten—masons never worked so hard—you've seen bees seething in and out of a honey-hole. The four walls were up by the time the first star was out. They put the timbers in the next day and they thatched the roof the day after that. It was the luckiest barn in the valley, never a winter without the huge rhythm of flails and showers of golden grain, and after that, winter ale and dancing on the swept floor.

The new schoolmaster took to calling Samuel 'Orpheus'.

'My name,' said Samuel stiffly, 'is Samuel Smith, Marsh, Rackwick, Hoy, Orkney, Scotland, if it's all the same to you. . . .' He considered that the schoolmaster was making a fool of him.

The laird's wife died, over in Hoy, at the Hall. The poor old gentleman, he shut himself from the light of the sun. No, he couldn't be bothered with the rent roll. No, he wouldn't speak to the fishermen. No, he wouldn't eat a thing, pheasant or trout. No whisky, thank you, no claret. Would they please leave him alone? Tell the factor not to come back again, the minister too. He sat in a room with the curtains drawn and he began to waste with grief like a snowman in April.

It was the laird's daughter, a tall proud ugly woman with loose strings in her neck, that sent for the fiddle. She sat Samuel of Marsh down in the library and she put a bottle full of malt whisky at his elbow. She poured a dram into the heavy cut crystal. Samuel first played a Scottish lament called 'Lochaber No More', a wild thing that fell through the great house like a black and white torrent among rocks and stones. Then he stopped for a while, drank more whisky, and began to play 'The Ploughman's Love for the Lady', shameless jigs that were usually never played but in the smithy on a Saturday night before the farm boys went courting. He was half way through the fourth chorus, when the door opened softly. The old laird came in like a ghost and sat down in the chair opposite Samuel. Samuel never let on he saw him. He filled up the cut crystal again and then began on the fifth verse. Samuel looked up once; the laird's old face was dimpling and smiling; no doubt he was remembering the nine illegitimates he had fathered on croft girls in every corner of the island in his young days. Samuel drank his next dram straight out of the bottle. Then he got to his feet and his bow went like lightning over the strings and he played 'The Tinkers' Wedding'.

The whisky bottle was empty then. Samuel went home.

Next morning the laird, his cheeks shining like apples,

presided at the district court. He acquitted Ikey the tinker of poaching in the burn, though half-a-dozen witnesses had seen him, including myself. Also he acquitted the young man and the girl caught kissing at the end of the Kirk during the Sabbath morning service. 'Love is a beautiful thing,' he told them. He found the three Flotta smugglers not guilty, though they turned up in court red in the face with French brandy, expecting heavy sentences. He sent no more flowers after that day to the lonely grave on the hillside. He lived for seven more years, a gentle courteous old man. The tinkers wept at the kirkyard gate the day of his funeral. Samuel had five shillings a week for life from him, and from his daughter after him.

It was an enchanted fiddle.

And yet, one season of madness, the people of this island smashed it to pieces, and along with the fiddle they broke a way of life that had gone on for centuries, and also, of course, they trampled like beasts on the proud heart of Samuel of Marsh.

This is what happened.

There was a young fellow in Hoy called Finlay Oman.

Finlay Oman was one of those men who dabble in everything, and are specially taken up with any novelty that comes along, a kind of magpie. He had been to the school here at Hamnavoe till he was fifteen, so when it became law that a register of births, marriages and deaths should be officially kept in every parish and not left to the whims of the Kirk session clerk, Finlay Oman was appointed to the job, to which were united the jobs of School Attendance Officer and Inspector of Poor. He gave up his loom—he had been a weaver— and he stood all day behind a desk with a pen in his hand. That in itself was enough to give him high standing among the crofters and fishermen, who thought of themselves as ignorant yokels. Few of them could read at that time. A man who could write with a pen in a ledger was half way to shedding the old salt and earth smells that they and their ancestors had been cursed with since Adam. It was the first year of compulsory education in Scotland, a thing—it was widely believed—that would make the peasant generations to come enlightened, respectable, prosperous, learned, free. Finlay Oman was also the first man in Hoy to own a spring cart with solid rubber wheels. He once went for a month's holiday to Edinburgh, a thing only the laird, the factor, and the minister had done up to that time. Everybody in the island made his own whisky in the secret places of the hills, far from excise officers. Finlay Oman had his sent to him from The White Horse in Hamnavoe, in bottles, duty paid. This for some reason was thought to be a very superior thing to do. Also he wore a collar and a tie and on Sundays a hard hat, like a black bowl with a rim on it turned upside down on his head.

I disliked the man very much.

Finlay Oman fiddled a bit at the barn dances. He played correctly enough but he was only a middling fiddler. The blessing was not in his strings.

One day something came in the boat from Hamnavoe for Finlay Oman, a black box that looked like the coffin of a hunchbacked dwarf. That afternoon loud cheap gaudy noises came from Finlay Oman's open door, raucous stuff, blocks of sound, it smashed the air apart for an hour or more. Music the like of it had never been heard in the island. The Hoy folk looked at each other in wonderment. That night Finlay Oman appeared in the smithy and told the crofters gathered round the forge that he had brought a new musical instrument to Orkney. It was called *the accordion*.

Every evening after that, for an hour or two, the Hoy folk were treated to this new music. You could recognize the traditional tunes through that startling noise, but to me it was all wrong, an outrage, like blasphemy screamed out in the Kirk. Mostly, however, Finlay Oman played new soft silly tunes. These, Finlay Oman let it be known, were recent ballads from the music-halls of London. He had them sent to him regularly by an Edinburgh music publisher.

The country folk looked at him admiringly. Finlay Oman, everyone said, was a credit to the island. They were lucky to have a man like that living among them. He was a new kind of hero, he was the Poor-Boy-who-had-Got-On.

To such an extent, in a few years, had education rotted the minds of the people.

One night that winter, just before Martinmas, a concert took place in the Hoy School. Among the folk down to perform were, of course, Samuel Smith of Marsh, Rackwick, on the fiddle, and Finlay Oman, registrar, on the accordion, and a few others, dancers, comics, and story-tellers, including myself.

Everybody from Hoy, Rackwick, Brims, Melsetter, Flotta, Risa, Fara and Osmundwall must have been in the school that night. The benches were crowded. They choked the door and they spread themselves against three walls. A good number of the men, and some women too, had been at the ale-house to get themselves in a proper mood for the concert. There was a good deal of boisterousness and—I thought—some menace too in the crowd as they waited for the concert to begin. It was a dangerous time of year, the threshold of winter.

The first performer, introduced by the master of ceremonies Mr Langskaill the factor, was Charlag the blacksmith. He bent seven horse shoes with his bare hands, one after the other, and he broke the last one with a noise like the clang of the Kirk bell. It was a thing that could be seen nearly every day in the smithy, so there wasn't much applause. Then it was my turn. I recited the story of The Two Women. It was a new story then, so I got my share of laughter.

Samuel of Marsh came in. He put the fiddle under his chin and he gave them 'Paulson's Escape from the Trows'—a lively reel, full of darkness, danger, pursuit, and in the end a wild surge of dawn and freedom. A few old men clapped their hands delightedly, but the younger folk heard the reel out in a stony silence. Samuel of Marsh bowed courteously and left the stage.

Ezra the Whaler was next. He sang 'The Ballad of Andrew Ross', a very lugubrious piece, and then went straight out of the school to the ale-house down the road for a shot of Barbados rum and was found drunk in the ditch next morning, to nobody's surprise.

A new item was announced—'Mister Finlay Oman and his accordion'. The young folk shouted and stamped their feet. Finlay Oman stood there, dark and smirking, with the instrument—huge labouring lung and clicking teeth—strapped to his chest. He played some of the latest ballads from London—'A Beautiful Picture in a Beautiful Frame of Gold', 'Tiny Seed of Love', 'I'll be Your Sweetheart'. A poetical silence followed the conclusion of this medley. A few women dabbed their cheeks with their handkerchiefs. Then they rose to him, and Finlay Oman left the stage in a tumult of rapture and acclaim.

When the enthusiasm had died down I was pushed on again. I gave them the story of The Fishing Boat. I thought I told it well that night. But I could sense an impatience in the audience, a hunger for novelty, progress, sophistication.

Old Samuel and his fiddle came on again. There were a few groans. He played 'The Swans of Stenness Loch'. The music brimmed out of his strings with all the purity and grace of those birds. Every curve, dip, and bend of the bow was itself a swan gesture. The melodies brimmed, they surged, they floated on their lucent reflections; they rose, a tumult of wings, and stormed into the sunset. . . .

Nothing happened. A few old men clapped uncertainly. The rest of the audience sat there as hard as stone.

Samuel of Marsh should have left the stage at that point, for now Finlay Oman was down on the programme for another selection of accordion music. Samuel didn't leave. He pushed the fiddle back among his whiskers and played 'The Davis Strait Whalers', 'The Harrayman and the Crab', 'The Witch of Quoybune'—great storms of sound that in better days had made every listener a hero.

All this while there was a rising groundswell of resentment in the hall, random shouts and abuse. Samuel had not heard it, or if he heard it he chose to ignore it. He began to play 'The Suleskerry Fishermen'. The opening notes smacked into us like a shower of salt spray. He got no further, for at this point Griselda of Trowieglen—may the Lord forgive her, the drunken disastrous old bitch!—leapt on to the stage. She shrieked at Samuel, then she hit him across the shoulders with her stick. The crowd was on its feet. They shouted for Griselda to hit him again! harder! again! Griselda hit him across the arm that held the fiddle. The fiddle fell. Strings shrieked from the floor. Then Griselda raised her foot and smashed it down on the instrument, and before the master of ceremonies could restore order Samuel's fiddle was a hundred bits of varnished wood and a tangle of wires.

Samuel smiled at Griselda. He bent forward and said something to her. Some folk say he kissed her. Then he turned and limped slowly off the stage like a wounded animal. A drunken howl followed him.

Samuel of Marsh was dead by the end of that same week. Fishermen broke down his door after no smoke had been seen coming from his chimney for three days. They found him slumped in his chair, a gentle silver smiling corpse.

Next morning six of us carried the old magician among the hills. I wish I was lying there beside him now.

*   *   *

'For the love of God,' said Drew the barman, 'drink up. The sergeant of police is coming up the pier.'

The hands of the clock stood at twenty minutes past ten.

Seven throats convulsed.

The Wireless Set

THE first wireless ever to come to the valley of Tronvik in Orkney was brought by Howie Eunson, son of Hugh the fisherman and Betsy.

Howie had been at the whaling in the Antarctic all winter, and he arrived back in Britain in April with a stuffed wallet and jingling pockets. Passing through Glasgow on his way home he bought presents for everyone in Tronvik—fiddle-strings for Sam down at the shore, a bottle of malt whisky for Mansie of the hill, a second-hand volume of Spurgeon's sermons for Mr Sinclair the missionary, sweeties for all the bairns, a meerschaum pipe for his father Hugh and a portable wireless set for his mother Betsy.

There was great excitement the night Howie arrived home in Tronvik. Everyone in the valley—men, women, children, dogs, cats—crowded into the but-end of the croft, as Howie unwrapped and distributed his gifts.

'And have you been a good boy all the time you've been away?' said Betsy anxiously. 'Have you prayed every night, and not sworn?'

'This is thine, mother,' said Howie, and out of a big cardboard box he lifted the portable wireless and set it on the table.

For a full two minutes nobody said a word. They all stood staring at it, making small round noises of wonderment, like pigeons.

'And mercy,' said Betsy at last, 'what is it at all?'

'It's a wireless set,' said Howie proudly. 'Listen.'

He turned a little black knob and a posh voice came out of the box saying that it would be a fine day tomorrow over England, and over Scotland south of the Forth-Clyde valley, but that in the Highlands and in Orkney and Shetland there would be rain and moderate westerly winds.

'If it's a man that's speaking', said old Hugh doubtfully, 'where is he standing just now?'

'In London,' said Howie.

'Well now,' said Betsy, 'if that isn't a marvel! But I'm not sure, all the same, but what it isn't against the scriptures. Maybe, Howie, we'd better not keep it.'

'Everybody in the big cities has a wireless,' said Howie. 'Even in Kirkwall and Hamnavoe every house has one. But now Tronvik has a wireless as well, and maybe we're not such clodhoppers as they think.'

They all stayed late, listening to the wireless. Howie kept twirling a second little knob, and sometimes they would hear music and sometimes they would hear a kind of loud half-witted voice urging them to use a particular brand of tooth-paste.

At half past eleven the wireless was switched off and everybody went home. Hugh and Betsy and Howie were left alone.

'Men speak,' said Betsy, 'but it's hard to know sometimes whether what they say is truth or lies.'

'This wireless speaks the truth,' said Howie.

Old Hugh shook his head. 'Indeed,' he said, 'it doesn't do that. For the man said there would be rain here and a westerly wind. But I assure you it'll be a fine day, and a southerly wind, and if the Lord spares me I'll get to the lobsters.'

Old Hugh was right. Next day was fine, and he and Howie took twenty lobsters from the creels he had under the Gray Head.

*　　*　　*

It was in the spring of the year 1939 that the first wireless set came to Tronvik. In September that same year war broke out, and Howie and three other lads from the valley joined the minesweepers.

That winter the wireless standing on Betsy's table became the centre of Tronvik. Every evening folk came from the crofts to listen to the nine o'clock news. Hitherto the wireless had been a plaything which discoursed Scottish reels and constipation advertisements and unreliable weather forecasts. But now the whole world was embattled and Tronvik listened appreciatively to enthusiastic commentators telling them that General Gamelin was the greatest soldier of the century, and he had only to say the word for the German Siegfried Line to crumble like sand. In the summer of 1940 the western front flared into life, and then suddenly no more was heard of General Gamelin. First it was General Weygand who was called the heir of Napoleon, and then a few days later Marshal Petain.

France fell all the same, and old Hugh turned to the others and said, 'What did I tell you? You can't believe a word it says'.

One morning they saw a huge gray shape looming along the horizon, making for Scapa Flow. 'Do you ken the name of that warship?' said Mansie of the hill. 'She's the *Ark Royal*, an aircraft carrier.'

That same evening Betsy twiddled the knob of the wireless and suddenly an impudent voice came drawling out. The voice was saying that German dive bombers had sunk the *Ark Royal* in the Mediterranean. 'Where is the *Ark Royal*?' went the voice in an evil refrain. 'Where is the *Ark Royal*? Where is the *Ark Royal*?'

'That man,' said Betsy 'must be the Father of Lies.'

Wasn't the *Ark Royal* safely anchored in calm water on the other side of the hill?

Thereafter the voice of Lord Haw-Haw cast a spell on the inhabitants of Tronvik. The people would rather listen to him than to anyone, he was such a great liar. He had a kind of bestial joviality about him that at once repelled and fascinated them; just as, for opposite reasons, they had been repelled and fascinated to begin with by the rapturous ferocity of Mr Sinclair's Sunday afternoon sermons, but had grown quite pleased with them in time.

They never grew pleased with William Joyce, Lord Haw-Haw. Yet every evening found them clustered round the portable radio, like awed children round a hectoring schoolmaster.

'Do you know,' said Sam of the shore one night, 'I think that man will come to a bad end?'

Betsy was frying bloody-puddings over a primus stove, and the evil voice went on and on against a background of hissing, sputtering, roaring and a medley of rich succulent smells.

Everyone in the valley was there that night. Betsy had made some new ale and the first bottles were being opened. It was good stuff, right enough; everybody agreed about that.

Now the disembodied voice paused, and turned casually to a new theme, the growing starvation of the people of Britain. The food ships were being sunk one after the other by the heroic U-boats. Nothing was getting through, nothing, nor a cornstalk from Saskatchewan nor a tin of pork from Chicago. Britain was starving. The war would soon be over. Then there would be certain pressing accounts to meet. The ships were going down. Last week the Merchant Navy was poorer by a half million gross registered tons. Britain was starving—

At this point Betsy, who enjoyed her own ale more than anyone else, thrust the hissing frying pan under the nose—so to speak—of the wireless, so that its gleam was dimmed for a moment or two by a rich blue tangle of bloody-pudding fumes.

'Smell that, you brute,' cried Betsy fiercely, 'smell that!'

The voice went on, calm and vindictive.

'Do you ken,' said Hugh, 'he canna hear a word you're saying.'

'Can he not?' said Sandy Omand, turning his taurine head from one to the other. 'He canna hear?'

Sandy was a bit simple.

'No,' said Hugh, 'nor smell either.'

After that they switched off the wireless, and ate the bloody-puddings along with buttered bannocks, and drank more ale, and told stories that had nothing to do with war, till two o'clock in the morning.

*   *   *

One afternoon in the late summer of that year the island postman cycled over the hill road to Tronvik with a yellow corner of telegram sticking out of his pocket.

He passed the shop and the manse and the schoolhouse, and went in a wavering line up the track to Hugh's croft. The wireless was playing music inside, Joe Loss and his orchestra.

Betsy had seen him coming and was standing in the door.

'Is there anybody with you?' said the postman.

'What way would there be?' said Betsy. 'Hugh's at the lobsters.'

'There should be somebody with you,' said the postman.

'Give me the telegram,' said Betsy, and held out her hand. He gave it to her as if he was a miser parting with a twenty-pound note.

She went inside, put on her spectacles, and ripped open

the envelope with brisk fingers. Her lips moved a little, silently reading the words.

Then she turned to the dog and said, 'Howie's dead.' She went to the door. The postman was disappearing on his bike round the corner of the shop and the missionary was hurrying towards her up the path.

She said to him, 'It's time the peats were carted.'

'This is a great affliction, you poor soul,' said Mr Sinclair the missionary. 'This is bad news indeed. Yet he died for his country. He made the great sacrifice. So that we could all live in peace, you understand.'

Betsy shook her head. 'That isn't it at all,' she said. 'Howie's sunk with torpedoes. That's all I know.'

They saw old Hugh walking up from the shore with a pile of creels on his back and a lobster in each hand. When he came to the croft he looked at Betsy and the missionary standing together in the door. He went into the outhouse and set down the creels and picked up an axe he kept for chopping wood.

Betsy said to him, 'How many lobsters did you get?'

He moved past her and the missionary without speaking into the house. Then from inside he said, 'I got two lobsters.'

'I'll break the news to him,' said Mr Sinclair.

From inside came the noise of shattering wood and metal.

'He knows already,' said Betsy to the missionary. 'Hugh knows the truth of a thing generally before a word is uttered.'

Hugh moved past them with the axe in his hand.

'I got six crabs forby,' he said to Betsy, 'but I left them in the boat.'

He set the axe down carefully inside the door of the outhouse. Then he leaned against the wall and looked out to sea for a long while.

'I got thirteen eggs,' said Betsy. 'One more than yesterday. That old Rhode Islander's laying like mad.'

The missionary was slowly shaking his head in the doorway. He touched Hugh on the shoulder and said, 'My poor man—'

Hugh turned and said to him, 'It's time the last peats were down from the hill. I'll go in the morning first thing. You'll be needing a cart-load for the Manse.'

The missionary, awed by such callousness, walked down the path between the cabbages and potatoes. Betsy went into the house. The wireless stood, a tangled wreck, on the dresser. She brought from the cupboard a bottle of whisky and glasses. She set the kettle on the hook over the fire and broke the peats into red and yellow flame with a poker. Through the window she could see people moving towards the croft from all over the valley. The news had got round. The mourners were gathering.

Old Hugh stood in the door and looked up at the drift of clouds above the cliff. 'Yes,' he said, 'I'm glad I set the creels where I did, off Yesnaby. They'll be sheltered there once the wind gets up.'

'That white hen,' said Betsy, 'has stopped laying. It's time she was in the pot, if you ask me.'

The Five of Spades

CHECK HARRA lived in the district of Swannay, Orkney, with his old mother, on the croft of Flosa. He was pledged to marry a girl in the village of Birsay called Clara Moar. The match was approved of by everyone concerned, including the laird and the minister, for Check Harra and Clara Moar were both respectable hard-working young people, and with moderate luck they could live happy at Flosa for many a year among their children and their children's children.

If Check Harra had one weakness it was that when he was a herdboy one summer he had learned to play card games in the smithy. He was the kind of player that the minister held up for a warning and an example—his whole nature was entirely changed with thumbing through that devil's book, the pack of cards, until at the end of an evening's gaming he humped in his corner little better than a beast or a troll.

One week-end Check Harra gambled away his mother's rent money in the stable of Smilders with the horsemen. Next morning he sold a sheep to the butcher in Dounby. The ewe was found to have the laird's nick in her ear.

Check was arrested by the bailiff that same night and taken to Kirkwall. He was put in the jail there until the sheriff had time to try the case. The day before the trial Check challenged his jailer, a man called Saul Mason, to a game of cards. In the course of the game Check struck down Saul Mason and took the keys from his belt and slipped the bolt and stepped out into the street.

It was winter. Check had no coat. He set out for Hamnavoe across the hills; he knew the road wasn't safe for him. He fell more than once in the deep snow drifts at Scorriedale. He had only one meal, a bowl of soup with tinkers in a quarry. 'Next time you're in Birsay,' he said to old Ezra the tinker, 'tell a lass there called Clara Moar that Check Harra will be back for her. . . .'

In Hamnavoe a ship called the *Anna* was anchored in the harbour. She was taking in fresh water before sailing for Nova Scotia with a cargo of tea, proof whisky, and porcelain.

The captain hadn't a full crew and he signed on Check Harra at once; Orkneymen were known to be good and reliable sailors. As the *Anna* was drifting out of the harbour next morning Check shouted across the still waters to the Hamnavoe men standing on their piers, 'When Clara Moar comes in from Birsay to the next Hamnavoe Market, tell her Check Harra's gone to America where all the gold is. It won't be long till he's home. All the sheep on Greenay Hill will be his then, tell Clara.'

Check was a good enough sailor. He worked hard and he held his grog and he got on well with the other men.

One night between decks when the guitar was silent Ole Olsen the Swede produced a pack of cards and began to play patience on the top of his sea chest. Another seaman and Check Harra stood watching him. A fourth seaman came off watch and proposed a hand of whist for penny stakes. The four of them squatted around the sea chest. Ole Olson shuffled and dealt.

Half an hour later he was bleeding from a cut on the side of his neck.

Check Harra was put in irons below deck and his red knife was brought on a tray to Captain Bellenger, and witnesses interrogated.

Next morning in latitude 60 while the crew stood ranged along the deck (Ole Olson with a bloody bandage round his neck) and the captain and officers and their

ladies watched from the bridge, Check Harra was cere-
monially stripped and tied to the grating. The bosun
stepped forward with the plaited thongs. It was like
laying the lash on a marble statue. Check Harra said
'Clara' once, between the first dozen and the second
dozen. There was as much blood at his lips as on his back
when the bosun finally cut him down and the jar of salt
was brought.

He was put ashore in Newfoundland.

At St. John's he signed on a Hull whaling boat. He had
handled nothing but a scythe and flail all his life; now he
took to the harpoon as if he had been bred among whales
and floes all his life. He was a strong man, and eye and
arm worked perfectly together.

Once, after weeks of fruitless drifting through the ice,
they sighted a whale. They launched the boat at the great
mild beast sporting in maelstroms and turmoils of its
own making. 'This whale is for Clara Moar,' said Check
Harra who was standing up in the bow. The whale rose
above them like St. Magnus Cathedral above a pony-
and-trap. Check launched his harpoon. The barb went
through the little eye of the whale and into the cavern of
its brain. It died in diminishing thunders and seaquakes.
It was the biggest whale killed in the Arctic that summer.
'Clara Moar' the men called her as they lashed her to the
side of the whaler and cut her to pieces and drew off the
barrels of oil. Check Harra got twenty-five sovereigns for
that piece of work. They said he could have been the
greatest whale-man in the Davis Straits.

A single evening in the saloon at St. John's, over a
game of jack-o-diamonds, ruined his career. The water-
front burned from midnight till dawn. The dozen whaling
skippers who never agreed about anything met in the
cabin of the *Tavistock* next morning and they swore that
Check Harra would never sail on any ship that they had

anything to do with. All that was found in the burnt-out saloon was a single playing card, the five of spades, and one of Check Harra's twenty-five sovereigns. The weeping landlord, a Chinaman, though he was entitled to keep both.

Check Harra worked his way slowly round to Hudson's Bay, nobody knew how.

He got a job in this trading station and that trading station, but he was never in one place for long. He was always on the move, here and there, restless as a mongrel dog. One day at the Red River Andrew Folster from Birsay saw him. Check Harra was breaking the ice on the other side of the river, trying to spear salmon. 'You from Orkney,' Check Harra cried to Andrew Folster, 'tell Clara Moar I might be a bit longer than I thought getting home. Tell her to hang on for a little while and she'll have a big house with servants in the Broad Street of Kirkwall and a pony-and-trap to drive about in.'

'I'll tell her that,' said Andrew Folster.

Check Harra walked half-way across the frozen river.

'I have a pack of cards here in my bag,' he said. 'How about a shuffle or two before you go on?'

'I'll give Clara Moar your message,' said Andrew Folster. He was a strict Presbyterian; he wouldn't so much as sully his mouth by mentioning cards.

'Just one game, for shilling stakes,' said Check Harra.

'Clara Moar will be told,' said Andrew Folster solemnly. He was going north at that time to join Doctor John Rae the explorer. In fact he never delivered that message in Birsay, for he died of pneumonia three months later at a place called Whiting Bay, but before he died he managed to tell it to Thorfinn Skea of Sanday. 'He sleeps the white sleep, this man,' said the Eskimos of Whiting Bay over the body of Andrew Folster. 'He was a man of fire three nights. Now he is a long cold man for as many nights as there are stars.' . . . There is a stone for Andrew Folster in the Birsay Kirkyard, in the Folsters' corner.

That was the last that was seen of Check Harra for a long time. He was reported to be living among the Indians. He was reported to have started a private trading post further west; he was doing well with skins, they said, and putting by money fast. A thousand Indians, it was said, worked for him. He was lord of an area as big as Britain, a white wilderness with here and there a reindeer herd on the move and at night the splendour of the Merry Dancers, swathes of heavy yellow silk swirling and rustling in the Arctic sky.

Once or twice he was seen in Fort Churchill, a morose figure behind his sledge and huskies. He would buy a couple of kegs of rum, silently read every line of the year-old newspapers (especially *The Orcadian*) and then shout his dogs into the west. He spoke to no-one more than was necessary.

Nobody knew anything for certain. Stories about Check Harra grew and accumulated, until at last he became a kind of legendary man on both sides of the Atlantic.

* * *

A fairground man with a guitar appeared at the Dounby Market in Orkney one August and sang a new ballad.

> *Check Harra was an Orkneyman*
> *Who sailed the Arctic Sea*
> *On a ship called the* Anna,
> *With a goodly company.*

> *Check Harra was an Orkneyman.*
> *He drank down buckets of ale.*

Beside the coasts of Greenland
He killed the king of the whales.

Check Harra was an Orkneyman,
The boldest ever seen.
A luckier gambler never laid
An ace upon a queen.

Check Harra was an Orkneyman
Who bought deer skins for rum.
When his chest is full of gold
Back to his sweetheart he'll come.

'That's right,' said Clara Moar who was standing in the crowd about the ballad singer. 'He'll be home next summer. Then the factor's fancy-woman better not sniff every time she passes me on the road. I'll be dropping wealth, the way a rose drops dew and bits of silk in the summer mornings. That was a good song, only the man might have put in a verse about the broken-hearted lass Check Harra left behind him in Orkney.' . . .

Clara Moar was then rounding out with her third child. A packman in Caithness called Fergus MacKenzie was said to be the father of it.

That ballad was sung for a long time in the islands.

But Check Harra never came home that summer, or the next summer, or the one after that.

In the imagination of the young folk of Orkney he became a hero. The wind shouted with his voice. His sweetheart was a part of the fertility of the fields. They were faithful with the fidelity of dawn and sunset.

*   *   *

In the autumn of 1862 a Hudson's Bay vessel called the *Albert* called at Hamnavoe. All the townsfolk from the senior magistrate to Ezra the hawker were at the pier

when the ship's boat came alongside. The governor of
Fort Churchill and John Rae the explorer and the master
of the *Albert* stepped ashore; also a few young country
men who had worked for a summer or two in Canada and
had come home to marry or, perhaps, rent a croft or a
fishing boat.

Last off came a complete family—a gnarled insigni-
ficant man and an Indian woman and four half-breed
children. The townsfolk hardly looked at them; the
arrival of men from the north-west with native concu-
bines was a common occurence. All eyes were on the
pioneers, explorers, empire builders.

Mr Louttit the senior magistrate made a long speech
of welcome.

In the middle of it the man and the woman and the four
children, shy as reindeer, moved up the pier and along
the street, out of sight.

*　　*　　*

The family got a hut at the back of the town to live in.
The man wasn't much good for any work—the north-
west had broken him. He was all twisted with rheumatics
like a wolf that had been a night and a day in a trap. The
roadmen would put a bit of tobacco in his hand at the
week-ends. Sometimes he got work at The White Horse
on a Saturday night, collecting the pewter mugs and
glasses from the tables and bringing them back to the
counter to be washed. Sometimes the ploughmen would
deal out cards for a hand to two of whist at the table next
the fire. On these occasions Maggie Marwick the land-
lady kept a hard eye on the old nor-west man as he went
about his duties. But nothing happened. What if the load
of pewter rattled on his tray whenever he passed the
ploughman's table, and one night when the game went

on for two hours he bit his lip till the blood came, like a seaman under the lash?

Check Harra had mastered the beast inside him at last.

The Indian woman could speak only a few words of English. Her feet were clumsy in the soft earth and teeming grass of the islands. Through the brief snows of winter she moved like a dark princess.

The four half-breed children quickly got used to the strange territory between hill and beach. Before that first winter was over they were at home with burns and fiddles and lupins and swans. The blond island children gathered them into their games. They had narrow dark faces and straight black gleaming hair and their eyes seemed always to be probing the horizon.

The ballad of Check Harra was sung no longer in the north.

As for Clara Moar, she remained a spinster. She had nine lovers in all, one for every separate cry in the cradle. 'It made a change,' said Clara Moar.

The Whaler's Return

FLAWS was at the Arctic whaling all summer and got back to Hamnavoe in the last week of August with seven pounds in gold, and a few shillings, tied in a belt round his middle under his shirt.

He said to Sabiston the harpooner, 'With this money I'm going to rent the croft of Breck and marry Peterina. I'll stay at home from now on. I'll work the three fields and maybe go to the lobsters when it's weather. I'll never see a whale or an iceberg again.'

Sabiston said, 'We'll go into The Arctic Whaler first and wash the salt out of our throats.'

In The Arctic Whaler they sat on barrels and drank ale. Then some other whaling men came in. They were all glad to be home. A few of them began to spend freely, buying rounds of rum for everyone in the bar. When it came to Flaws's turn, he bought rum for everyone too. Then, alarmed at his extravagance—he had fractured one of his sovereigns to buy the round of rum and the loose copper and silver lay in his hand like so much cold mud and snow—he rose to his feet and said to Sabiston, 'Now I'm going to walk home to Birsay.'

Before he went, Phimister of the *Skua* sang 'The Harray Crab'. The north-west men roared out the chorus.

Phimister sang the song well. Everyone crowded about him with drink, Flaws also.

*   *   *

Flaws hoisted his box on his shoulder. He left The Arctic Whaler at ten in the morning and set out for

115

Birsay. At the north end of Hamnavoe he saw that there
was a new ale-house called The White Horse. It must
have opened for the first time during the summer.

He put his head through the door and saw a few
farmers sitting round the fire drinking. The barmaid
was standing at a mirror twisting her yellow hair at
the back of her head. At last she got a fine burnished
knot on it and drove a pin through to hold it in
place.

Flaws hadn't seen a woman for six months. He went
in and asked for a mug of ale.

'We only sell whisky here,' said the girl, 'threepence
a glass.'

'A glass of whisky then,' said Flaws.

He thought it might be the last chance he would ever
have to speak to a pretty girl. Peterina was good and
hard-working, but rather ugly.

Flaws stood at the bar and drank his whisky. The four
farmers sat round the fire saying little. It was Wednesday in Hamnavoe, the day they drove in their beasts to
sell at the Mart.

'Do you do much trade in The White Horse?' said
Flaws to the barmaid.

'We welcome only the better sort of person here,' said
the girl, 'the quiet country men, not the ruffians and
tramps from the herring boats and the whalers. And of
course the office workers too, and business people.
We're always very busy in the evening after the shops
and offices close. No fighting scum from the boats ever
cross the threshold of The White Horse.' Out of her
pretty mouth she spat on the stone floor.

Flaws was glad he was wearing his decent suit of
broadcloth, the one his old mother always packed in
mothballs at the bottom of his chest for departures and
home-comings.

He ordered two glasses of whisky, one for the barmaid. She smiled at him sweetly. They touched rims till the glasses made a small music and the whisky trembled into yellow circles. Flaws was transported. He longed to touch her burnished head. Given time, solitude, and another dram or two, he could well imagine himself kissing her across the bar.

'I haven't seen you in The White Horse before,' said the barmaid. 'What is your occupation, sir?'

'God forgive me for telling a lie,' said Flaws to himself. Then he squared his shoulders and said, 'I only visit the islands now and then. I'm a commercial traveller. I travel for earthenware and china.'

The barmaid glittered at him with eyes, teeth, hair, rings.

The door opened and Small the lawyer's clerk tiptoed in, his drunken nose (Flaws thought) redder than ever. He went up to the bar slowly, eyeing Flaws the way a hunter eyes his quarry. 'If it isn't Flaws!' he cried at last. 'If it isn't my old friend! And did you catch many whales at Greenland, eh? I can smell the blubber and the oil with you. I warrant you have a fine pile of sovereigns in your pocket. You're the first seaman ever to get into The White Horse.'

Flaws could have killed the little drunken clerk at that moment. The barmaid was suddenly looking at him with eyes as cold as stones.

Flaws hoisted his box on his shoulder and made for the door without a word. His pocket was heavy with more silver and copper; he had broken another sovereign in The White Horse. He stood, hot with shame and resentment, on the road outside.

'A commercial traveller!' cried Small the lawyer's clerk at the bar. Suddenly the interior of The White Horse was loud with merriment, the deep bass laughter of the farmers mingling with the falsetto mirth of the lawyer's clerk and the merry tinkle of the barmaid.

Flaws walked on towards Birsay, red in the face.

*　　*　　*

'Thank God to be clear of Hamnavoe at least', said Flaws to himself. There were forty pubs and ale-houses in the one long twisting street of the town. A good many of the returned whalers would have visited them all by the week-end. By Monday morning Sabiston and a few others wouldn't have a sixpence left. Flaws considered that he had done well, only drinking in two howffs.

It was a long road, sixteen miles, to Birsay. The day was fine, with a clear cold sky. Oats were ripening in a field at the end of the town. The rum and whisky put a rhythm in his step. How grand it was to be walking on the firm roads of home once more, not lurching about on the frozen deck of a whaling ship, with death everywhere round you, in berg and whale and unquiet water, and worst of all in the sudden knives of the drunk dice-players at midnight. Flaws had had nothing to do with them. His bible had kept him safe. He had read a chapter every night in his hammock before turning over to sleep, while the little ivory cubes rattled wickedly on the lid of a sea chest.

In Sandwick Flaws began to feel hungry.

An old woman called Bella Jean Bews kept a lodging house at Yesnaby, half a mile off the road. Flaws thought he might get a plate of salt fish there, enough to keep him going.

A rich smell met him in the door. Bella Jean Bews had been both baking and brewing. A tall pile of new bannocks smoked on her table, and a kirn beside the fire seethed with ale.

'Yes,' said Bella Jean Bews, 'come in, boy. I'll give

thee something to eat.' She put two boiled crabs in front of him on the bare table and a thick hot buttered bannock. 'Help theeself,' she said.

Flaws ate till there was a comfortable tightness across his stomach. 'Have you such a thing as a drop of milk?' said Flaws.

'Better than milk,' said Bella Jean Bews. She dipped a wooden bowl in the kirn and brought it, brimming with green ale, to Flaws, 'Drink that, boy,' she said, 'that'll help thee on thee way. Are thu gang far?'

'To Birsay,' said Flaws, and tasted some of the ale. It was a raw sweet unfinished brew.

'A fair walk,' said Bella Jean Bews. 'Drink up, boy.'

Suddenly she leaned forward and put her face close to his. 'Is thee name Flaws?' she said.

'It is,' said Flaws.

'And thu've been at the Davis Strait since April,' she said, 'at the whales?'

'Yes,' said Flaws.

'And thu're contracted to be married at harvest to Peterina Gold of Fadoon?'

'That's a fact,' said Flaws.

'Well,' said Bella Jean Bews, 'I'm glad to see thee. Peterina's father, old Jock Gold the roadman, was kicked on the head with a horse the week after midsummer. He lay down in the ditch with the red hoof mark on him. The peat-cutters from the hill found him there. They took him home to Fadoon in a cart. Peterina said nothing when they carried her father into the house. She didn't even have a drink of whisky to give to the peatcutters. It's a poor house thu're marrying into. Peterina put a shawl over her head and she walked over the hills here to Yesnaby. The two of us made for Birsay at once to get there before it was dark. There was Jock Gold on the floor, with a red wound the shape of a horse-shoe on his skull. Peterina took a long gray shirt from the chest under the bed, Jock's shroud that his mother had sewed for him as soon as he was a grown man, for nobody can tell when death will come. Then I washed the body and I put the gray shirt on it and I folded his hands. We lit the lamp then—it was dark by this time. Peterina wrote in the big bible in the window, "John Gold, killed by a horse the week after midsummer." There was little in the cupboard, some oatmeal and a sup of milk. It's a poor woman thu'll get for a wife. Peterina never shed one tear for her father. "He was a queer bitter man," she said. "The house'll be sweeter without him." . . . Later, near midnight, she turned to me and she said, "I have no money to pay you for your services this night. Forgive me. But Andrew Flaws will pay you when he gets back from the whales, if he ever gets back, for we see how dangerous life is, even for a roadman." . . . I stayed with her all that night. On my way home, at first light next morning, I knocked at the gravedigger's door.'

'God save him,' said Flaws.

'Amen,' said Bella Jean Bews. 'Drink up. There's plenty of ale. I have another crab in the pot.'

'Just a mug of ale,' said Flaws. 'He was a queer twisted bitter man. Peterina has had a poor life with him this seven years past.'

'That's in God's hands,' said Bella Jean Bews. 'Don't drink so fast. It's very strong ale. My fee for the shrouding is half a guinea.'

Flaws took a sovereign out of his belt and laid it on the table.

'There,' he said. 'I want no change.'

'For your wedding,' said Bella Jean Bews, 'you'll be wanting a serving-woman. And soon after that, no doubt, you'll be needing a midwife for Peterina. I'll be glad to come.'

'Yes,' said Flaws. 'Give me a last mug of strong ale, then I'll go.'

*   *   *

Flaws walked on through the parish of Sandwick, his feet easy on the road, the box on his shoulder as light as if it was stuffed with larks' feathers. Some of the oat-fields he passed were still green, others were touched with the first gold. They whispered densely round him in the stillness; the countryside was one huge conspiracy for the benefit of bewintered man. Then, in a freshet of wind, deep surges went through the oatfields, and the barley undulated and shimmered like new silk. It would be a good harvest. He hurried on; next year he himself, the new crofter of Breck, would take part in this ritual of the corn, the cycle of birth, love, death, resurrection. He hurried on. An awkward old man had died up at Fadoon. Soon Peterina would write in the black bible, 'Andrew Flaws and Peterina Gold, married at the end of harvest', and afterwards, in a weak hand, 'Andrew John Gold Flaws, first son to Andrew and Peterina Flaws, born in the time of hay.' . . . So life went on. The seed was buried, the ripe corn fell, bread was broken. He hurried along the road to Birsay. There were six ale-houses be-tween Sandwick and Birsay. Flaws decided that he would visit none of them. The only person he wanted to see now was Peterina. He hurried on past Scarth's ale-house and Wylie's ale-house (though there was a sound of bag-pipes from there) and Spence's ale-house.

At the gate of Halcro's ale-house, as he was hurrying past, a hand shot out of the bushes and gripped Flaws by the arm. He almost dropped his sea-chest with shock. A grizzled sly laughing face was stuck into his. It was Halcro himself, the landlord.

'Andrew Flaws,' he cried. 'Welcome home, Andrew

Flaws. I'm glad to see thee, Andrew Flaws. What's all this hurry, Andrew Flaws? Andrew Flaws, thu must have a drink with me.'

'No', said Flaws, still in a trance of love and labour and fulfilment. 'No.'

'What kind of a way is that to speak, Andrew Flaws?' said Halcro. 'Come on in. The whales are all dead and men must live and rejoice.'

'No,' said Flaws.

Halcro dragged him by the arm towards the ale-house. 'Men,' he yelled to the drinkers inside, 'look who's here, Andrew Flaws. Andrew Flaws is home again. He's wanting to celebrate, Andrew Flaws.'

Flaws struggled like a fly in honey.

Suddenly the door of Halcro's ale-house was crammed with faces and pewter mugs.

'Andrew Flaws!' they all cried, and there was a tilting of heads and a steeper tilting of mugs and a working of throats. 'Welcome home, Andrew Flaws,' said a score of frothy beards.

So there was no escape for Flaws at Halcro's. He drank with the Sandwick men till the ale-house plunged and swayed like a Lofoten whaler in a gale. Pewter clashed and foamed round him. He was clapped on the shoulder a hundred times.

'A drink for Andrew Flaws,' cried old Halcro.

Flaws took a sovereign out of his belt to repay their hospitality. The sovereign was quickly broken up, first into florins, then into sixpences, then into pennies, and all the fragments flowed back into Halcro's till.

Soon the ale ran out and they all began to drink Norwegian spirits, aquavit.

Late in the afternoon Flaws said seriously to Peter of Skaill who was standing beside him, 'Now I don't feel as if I was on a whaling boat, it's more as if I was in the belly of a whale, wound in guts. Peter, I must go.'

He made a great lurch between the barrel and the door.

The noise of the ale-house faded.

He found himself on the road again, alone, a bewildered Jonah.

*   *   *

'What I want to know, sir, is this,' said Flaws. 'Was he properly buried?'

'No question of it,' said Mr Selly the minister. 'I performed the ceremony myself. I said a prayer in the house and another prayer at the graveside. Also I read an appropriate passage from holy writ, *Man goeth to his long home*. Death is a great mystery. There is, though, Andrew, one small matter, the funeral was conducted with maimèd rites, as Hamlet described it. Neither the minister's fee nor the gravedigger's fee was paid. Well, of course, we must expect such omissions from time to time. In this case the girl is poor. The omissions can always be repaired when circumstances improve.'

'How much do the fees come to?' said Flaws.

'Five shillings,' said Mr Selly, 'a half-crown for the gravedigger and the same amount for me.'

Flaws brought a handful of silver and copper out of his pocket. He picked out a large crown piece and set it on the manse table. 'There,' he said.

'Splendid,' said Mr Selly. He unlocked a metal box on the sideboard and put the crown piece inside. 'If they were all like you, Andrew.'

'How much is a wedding fee?' said Flaws.

'Half-a-crown,' said Mr Selly.

Flaws picked a half-crown out of the heaped treasure in his fist and laid it on the table. 'I'll be marrying Peterina Gold of Fadoon at the end of harvest,' he said.

'Very good,' said Mr Selly. 'I'm glad to hear it. You will have to see the Session Clerk, of course, Mr Work, so that the banns can be read in church. Splendid.' He rattled the half-crown into the cash box and locked it. 'I think we can dispense with receipts. We trust each other, don't we? Andrew, I think this calls for a little celebration.' He opened the cupboard door and took out a bottle and two glasses.

Flaws said, 'I want to get to Fadoon before it's dark.'

'Of course,' said Mr Selly. 'I understand. But this, Andrew, is the very best brandy, cognac. Andrew, I know you will tell nobody about this, but there was a French ship in the bay one night last month in the dark of the moon. Twenty-one kegs of brandy were taken off her, unbeknown to the excise, plus a huge quantity of tobacco. Twenty-one kegs. Through an agency that I shall not divulge, one of those kegs found its way to the Manse'. He winked at Flaws, then carefully filled two glasses with the brandy.

'Andrew,' he said, raising his glass, 'may your marriage be long and prosperous. Peterina is a good girl, and poverty is no crime.'

'Thank you,' said Flaws, and gulped the foreign stuff down. Tears stood in his eyes. He got to his feet. 'Goodnight, minister.'

'Goodnight, Andrew,' said Mr Selly. 'It's a good spirit, isn't it? I'm glad you're home again. Mr Partridge-Simpson the laird is keeping the croft of Breck for you. I spoke to him one day last week. We'll be seeing you in your pew on Sunday as usual? I hope so.'

*　　*　　*

In the flagstone quarry a mile past the Manse the tinkers were holding some kind of celebration. A large fire was burning, and round it the tinkers sat in groups. From time to time one of them gave vent to a wild cry, then there was silence again. A young girl went round with a jug, pouring drink into their cups.

It was dark on the road. Flaws felt very tired, as if he had walked a hundred miles since morning, as if he had made a wide detour round the real world and was now wandering deeper and deeper into the heart of fantasy.

He left the road and crouched among the bushes in the darkness, watching the tinkers' ritual.

It was a wedding.

Will and Mary sat at opposite ends of a large flat stone that had been hewn out of the quarry a long time ago. They were in their usual rags, except that clean white handkerchiefs were tied round their throats. Between them sat Ezra, the chief of the clan, as solemn as a king or a priest. Tonight he was the celebrant at the mysteries.

An old woman, Heather, stood in front of them, a little to one side, her voice rising every now and again in a passion of denunciation.

The other tinkers sat well behind, in dark intent groups. The only moving figures was the girl who carried round the jug of spirits.

'You, Will,' cried Heather, 'stole three hens from the farm of the Glebe in April and in the month of June you took a sack of peats from Mucklehouse and you took a tin of syrup from the grocer's van in Dounby on the Thursday of the Agricultural Show. Didn't you poach salmon out of the burn at Strathnaver in Sutherlandshire? You did. And you are nowise fit to be the husband of this good girl, Mary.'

'Answer, Will,' said Ezra.

'Things happen,' said Will, 'both good and evil. I will keep bread in Mary's mouth.'

'I take him for my man,' said Mary.

'It is well spoken,' said Ezra.

Everybody drank out of their cups, except Will, Mary, and the old woman, the devil's advocate.

Flaws peered through the screen of branches. He felt a tap on his shoulder. The dark girl, the cup-bearer, stood beside him, holding out a mug with liquor in it. She smiled at him, then softly returned to the barrel to refill her jug. Flaws took a deep drink. His mouth and throat were so scoured with rum, whisky, ale, aquavit, and brandy that this stuff went down as tasteless as water; but he felt a slow dark smoulder in his stomach.

The old woman suddenly screamed out, 'Will, didn't you get drunk at the Kirkwall Market and fight with a Norwegian sailor in the Laverock, and didn't they keep you in jail all that week-end? Didn't you get drunk at the Harvest Home in Canisby, Caithness, and break the fiddle over Gunn the fiddler's head because Gunn was playing the reel wrong? Weren't you drunk three times between the Hamnavoe Market and Hallowe'en, and again four times between Hallowe'en and Hogmanay? And you shall not be the husband of this good girl, Mary.'

'Answer,' said Ezra.

'Things happen,' said Will, 'both good and bad. I will keep a shawl about her shoulders.'

'And I take him for my man,' said Mary.

'It is well spoken,' said Ezra.

The tinkers drank, all except Will, Mary, and old Heather. The girl was beside Flaws once more. The spirit went into his cup, a tiny sweet music. Then she was off like a shadow.

The old woman began again, beating the air with her fist. 'Will,' she cried, 'what were you after the age of fourteen? Not a virgin. You tore the buttons off Liz's dress and you laid Dolina down in a wet ditch and you went naked at midnight into Belle's tent the time her man Sam was away at the rag gathering. The girl Seena in Dounby has a bairn the very spit of you. You kissed the laird's servant lass at the end of the stable door—the mark of the factor's whip is still on your throat from that on-carry. You must not be the husband of this good girl Mary.'

Heather's shrieks echoed from wall to wall of the quarry.

'Answer', said Ezra.

'Things happen,' said Will, 'both good and bad. I will light fires for her in winter.'

'And I take him for my man,' said Mary.

'It is well spoken,' said Ezra.

The tinkers raised their mugs. The dark girl poked the fire and a flame roared high. Then she slipped behind the bush with her jug and filled Flaws's cup. This time she did not look at him.

Old Heather began to speak again, but now in a gentle voice. 'You, Mary. I will speak against you. With most brides it's no trouble to say a lot, with their whoring and garbing and gossiping. But there's little against you, Mary. You lost a bag of pins, a shillingsworth, at the Dounby Market the year before last. You scorched a rabbit once that was stewing over the fire. The solder came off a tin pail you made for the Holm doctor. So you will not be the wife of this good man Will.'

'Answer,' said Ezra.

'Things happen, both good and bad,' said Mary. 'I will carry his children proudly.'

'I take her for my wife,' said Will.

'It is well spoken,' said Ezra.

The tinkers rose to their feet, drank, cheered, and threw the dregs of their whisky into the fire. Then they all sat down again.

Quickly the girl filled up every cup in the quarry. This

time she did not carry her jug over to Flaws. She stooped and whispered in the ear of Angus, a young powerful tinker, and pointed to the bush where the intruder squatted unseen.

'Now,' said Ezra, 'the bucket.'

Old Heather placed a tin pail between the fire and the ceremonial stone. Will rose from his place and went over to the pail. He loosed his breeches and urinated into it. Then it was Mary's turn. She hoisted up her skirt, squatted over the pail, and urinated into it. Solemnly Ezra lifted the pail and swilled it seven times in sunward circles. 'Whoever can separate this water,' he cried, 'can separate this man Will and this woman Mary.' Then he emptied out the mingled urine on the quarry floor.

Will and Mary kissed each other.

The tinkers danced, yelled, shouted, rose to their feet. A fiddle began to play. Dancing broke out all over the quarry. A dog in a nearby farm barked. Ezra and old Heather circled each other, slow and grave. The ritual bearing round of drink was forgotten; now the tinkers held their mouths under the dripping tap of the barrel and staggered away. The feet beat on and the dance grew wilder. Where was the beautiful cup-bearer? Flaws wanted to dance with her. He wanted to hear the sound of her voice. He wanted to ask her why she had bypassed him on her last circuit and why she had whispered so secretly to Angus. He wanted to kiss her before he gave his kisses to Peterina for ever. He rose from the heart of the bush and wandered uncertainly towards the flames and the din. There she was, putting a sea-bleached board into the fire, her bare arm rosy in the flame. He made for her. The fiddle screamed in his ear. Ezra passed his reeking pipe to Heather. 'Girl,' said Flaws. She turned a blank cold face on him.

A hand clawed and tore.

Then the black snarling wave was all about him.

* * *

He woke in a ditch below Fadoon, in broad daylight, a mile and more from the tinkers' quarry.

Painfully he got to his feet. His bones creaked. Water ran out of his sleeve. His tongue lay in his mouth like a filthy rag.

His first thought was for his money. His fingers groped under his shirt. There were two sovereigns left in his belt. Out of his pocket he brought twelve shillings in silver and a few coppers. A surge of relief went through him. He would at least be able to pay the first half year's rent for Breck, two guineas.

He walked between two fields to Fadoon. The last green was gone from the oats now; the harvest burnish was on every blade. There was a curl of smoke from the roof and the door stood open. He bowed his head under the lintel and went in. Peterina was sitting at her spinning wheel.

'Peace to this place,' said Flaws.

'You're back from the whales, Andrew Flaws', said Peterina.

'Yes,' he said.

'You're in better shape than I expected,' said Peterina. 'There are thirty-four ale-houses in the town of Hamnavoe and sixteen ale-houses on the road between Hamnavoe and Birsay. Some men from the ships are a long time getting home.'

'I have the rent for the croft of Breck,' said Flaws, 'and a shilling or two besides.'

'We move in in November,' said Peterina. She went over to the cupboard and brought out a jug and a bannock. 'Bring over your chair to the table,' she said. 'Here's some bread and ale.'

While Flaws was eating, Peterina said, 'There's little news in the parish. My father was killed by a horse in the month of June. God forgive me for speaking ill of the dead, but it's been a quiet house since then. A quiet house but a bare house. I've had to live on the parochial poor fund since the funeral. With the shame of that, I don't show my face in the public. I wasn't able to pay any of the death money, neither the shrouding fee nor the fee for the digging of the grave nor the minister's fee.'

'I saw to all that on my way home,' said Flaws. 'Everything is paid.'

'That was a good thing you did, Andrew Flaws,' said Peterina.

'And the wedding fee is paid too,' said Flaws.

'That will be in the last week of September,' said Peterina. 'I will try to be a good wife to you, Andrew Flaws. Before that time I must make a blanket for the bed, and a christening shawl for the first bairn, and two shrouds, one for you and one for me, for no man can tell the day or the hour, and we must be ready at all times.' The wheel went round and the new gray wool slid between her fingers.

'I tarred the boat down at the beach,' said Peterina. 'You'll fish until such time as we reap our first harvest at Breck.'

'Yes,' said Flaws.

'There was a wedding last night at the tinkers' camp in the quarry,' said Peterina. 'It was a wild celebration. I heard fiddles at three o'clock in the morning.'

'Yes,' said Flaws. He drank the last of the ale. It was the sweetest drink he had ever tasted. 'I think I'll sleep for an hour or two,' he said, 'then I'll maybe catch a few haddocks, before sunset. The laird will be wanting harvesters tomorrow or the day after.'

The Bright Spade

THAT winter the gravedigger was the busiest man in the island.

They got the thin harvest in and then the wind squatted in the east, a winter witch, and blew the island gray with her breath.

James of Moss died in the last week of October. Jacob dug his grave and got a bottle of whisky for it from the widow of Moss. This death was not unexpected. James of Moss had been ill with dropsy all summer; he had clung to life like the last tattered leaf on a branch.

The gravedigger had hardly sobered up when he was called to the house of Maria of Graystones. There Maria lay as stiff and pale as a candle. He dug her grave near the wall of the kirk. Maria's nephew gave him a goose.

There was not much food in the island even at the beginning of winter, and the ale was sour and thin.

In early November the laird's youngest son was thrown from his horse at the bridge and broke his neck. 'This will need a deep grave,' said Jacob. He threw up many fine white bones, the laird's ancestors, with his spade. The laird gave him half a guinea, and a dram both before and after the funeral.

Late November and early December brought death to Samuel Ling the fisherman, Jean the wife of Ebenezer of Ness, and the boy with the hare lip from the Quarry. They were all poor people and Jacob got nothing at all for his work but a box of coarse tobacco snuff from Ebenezer of Ness. 'I suppose I'll be glad of somebody to bury me when my time comes,' said Jacob, and sneezed heroically for a month till the snuff was finished.

It was a hard winter, and nobody expected most of the old people and the sickly people to see the spring.

At harvest Kirstie had given birth to a daughter, just three months after she had married Amos of the Glebe. Kirstie and Amos raged at each other so much, both before and after the birth, that there wasn't a bowl or a dish unbroken in the cupboard. In the season of snow and small fires the infant breathed her last; she died the week before Christmas. Jacob dug a small grave in the east corner of the kirkyard. He got a shilling from Kirstie and a pocket-full of potatoes from Amos. The day after the funeral Kirstie left Amos and went back to her parents' house. She never lived with Amos again.

The day after New Year a Dutch ship went ashore at the Red Head. Unfortunately the ship had no cargo; she was in ballast, bound for Labrador. Seven bodies were found on the shore next morning. The minister asked Jacob to dig one large grave for the foreigners.

'Who will pay my fee?' said Jacob.

'I don't know that,' said the minister, 'for the next-of-kin are in the Low Countries.'

In the end Jacob agreed to dig their grave for three spars of timber from the wrecked ship and half a barrel of oil out of the hold.

That month the food was very low in girnal and kirn. Before the beginning of February Abraham of Corse died, and the cripple girl from the Glebe. Jacob got nothing for the girl. The widow of Corse gave him Abraham's brass watch. Abraham was ninety-four years old, and the girl from the Glebe sixteen.

One night there was a meeting in the ale-house. All the men of the island were there. They took counsel together about the impending famine. That same morning the old man of Cornquoy who lived alone, the fiddler, had been found dead in his chair, after he had been missed for a week. They broke down his door. The young dog was gnawing at the corpse's thigh. Jacob got his fiddle the night he shrouded him, though he knew nothing about music. The fiddle, once a sweet brimming shell, hung at Jacob's wall like a shrivelled chrysalis. The old fiddler was as light as a bird to handle. He needed a narrow grave.

'The meal and the meat are done in the island,' said Harald of Ness at the meeting. 'I've eaten nothing myself but a handful of cold potatoes every day for the past week. My suggestion is this, that seven of the strongest men among us cross between the hills to the shore and get a large supply of limpets and dulse from the rocks at low tide.'

The men agreed that it would be necessary to do that.

The seven men chosen set off at dawn the next day. They were Harald of Ness, Adam of Skarataing, Ezekiel of the Burn, Thomas and Philip of Graystones, Simon the blacksmith, and Walter of Muce. That same morning the worst blizzard of winter descended, great swirling blankets of snow out of the east. Tinkers saw the seven men between the hills going towards the shore, like a troop of spectres. They were never seen again till their bodies were dug from the drifts a week later.

For the second time that winter Jacob laid seven men together in the kirkyard. This time he would accept no payment at all for his services – 'for,' said he, 'it seems I have done better this winter than anybody else in the island . . .'.

In March Francis Halcro the coughing sailor who had been with John Paul Jones in the American Wars died at Braebuster. Jacob buried him for his set of Nantucket harpoons.

And then men brought out ploughs, harness, harrows. The implements were dull and rusty after the hard winter. Jacob's spade, on the other hand, was thin and bright with much employment. 'God grant,' he said to the spade, putting it away in his shed, 'that I won't be needing you again till after the shearing and the lobster fishing and the harvest.'

Tartan

THEY anchored the *Eagle* off the rock, in shallow water, between the horns of a white sandy bay. It was a windy morning. Behind the bay stretched a valley of fertile farms.

'We will visit those houses,' said Arnor the helmsman. Olaf who was the skipper that voyage said he would bide on the ship. He had a poem to make about rounding Cape Wrath that would keep him busy.

Four of the Vikings—Arnor, Havard, Kol, Sven—waded ashore. They carried axes in their belts.

Gulls rose from the crag, circled, leaned away to the west.

The first house they came to was empty. But the door stood open. There was a shirt drying on the grass and a dog ran round them in wild noisy circles. Two sheep were tethered near the back wall.

'We will take the sheep as we return,' said Havard.

Between this house and the next house was a small burn running fast and turbid after the recent rain. One by one they leapt across it. Kol did not quite make the far bank and got his feet wet. 'No doubt somebody will pay for this,' he said.

'That was an unlucky thing to happen,' said Sven. 'Everything Kol has done this voyage has been wrong.'

Another dog came at them silently from behind, a tooth grazed Arnor's thigh. Arnor's axe bit the dog to the backbone. The animal howled twice and died where he lay.

In the second house they found a fire burning and a pot of broth hanging over it by a hook. 'This smell makes my nostrils twitch,' said Sven. 'I am sick of the salted beef and raw fish that we eat on board the *Eagle*.'

They sat round the table and put the pot of soup in the centre. While they were supping it Sven raised his head and saw a girl with black hair and black eyes looking at them from the open door. He got to his feet, but by the time he reached the door the girl was three fields away.

They finished the pot of broth. 'I burnt my mouth,' said Kol.

There were some fine woollen blankets in a chest under the bed. 'Set them out,' said Arnor, 'they'll keep us warm at night on the sea.'

'They are not drinking people in this valley,' said Havard, who was turning everything upside down looking for ale.

They crossed a field to the third house, a hovel. From the door they heard muttering and sighing inside. 'There's breath in this house,' said Kol. He leapt into the middle of the floor with a loud berserk yell, but it might have been a fly buzzing in the window for all the attention the old woman paid to him. 'Ah,' she was singing over the sheeted dead child on the bed, 'I thought to see you a shepherd on Morven, or maybe a fisherman poaching salmon at the mouth of the Naver. Or maybe you would be a man with lucky acres and the people would come from far and near to buy your corn. Or you might have been a holy priest at the seven altars of the west.'

There was a candle burning at the child's head and a cross lay on his breast, tangled in his cold fingers.

Arnor, Havard, and Sven crossed themselves in the door. Kol slunk out like an old dog.

They took nothing from that house but trudged uphill to a neat gray house built into the sheer brae.

At the cairn across the valley, a mile away, a group of plaided men stood watching them.

At the fourth door a voice called to them to come in. A thin man was standing beside a loom with a half-made web in it. 'Strangers from the sea,' he said, 'you are welcome. You have the salt in your throats and I ask you to accept ale from Malcolm the weaver.'

They stood round the door and Malcolm the weaver poured horns of ale for each of them.

'This is passable ale,' said Havard. 'If it had been sour, Malcolm the weaver, we would have stretched you alive on your loom. We would have woven the thread of eternity through you.'

Malcolm the weaver laughed.

'What is the name of this place?' said Arnor.

'It is called Durness,' said Malcolm the weaver. 'They are good people here, except for the man who lives in the tall house beyond the cairn. His name is Duncan, and he will not pay me for the cloth I wove for him last winter, so that he and his wife and his snovelly-nosed children could have coats when the snow came.'

'On account of the average quality of your ale, we will settle matters with this Duncan,' said Arnor. 'Now we need our cups filled again.'

They stayed at Malcolm the weaver's house for an hour and more, and when they got up to go Kol staggered against the door. 'Doubtless somebody will pay for this,' he said thickly.

They took with them a web of cloth without asking leave of Malcolm. It was a gray cloth of fine quality and it had a thick green stripe and a thin brown stripe running up and down and a very thick black stripe cutting across it horizontally. It was the kind of Celtic weave they call tartan.

'Take it, take it by all means,' said Malcolm the weaver.

'We were going to take it in any case,' said Sven.

'Tell us,' said Havard from the door, 'who is the girl in Durness with black hair and black eyes and a cleft chin?'

'Her name is Morag,' said Malcolm the weaver, 'and she is the wife of John the shepherd. John has been on the hill all week with the new lambs. I think she is lonely.'

'She makes good soup,' said Arnor. 'And if I could get hold of her for an hour I would cure her loneliness.'

It took them some time to get to the house of Duncan because they had to support Kol who was drunk. Finally they stretched him out along the lee wall of the house. 'A great many people will suffer,' said Kol, and began to snore.

The Gaelic men were still standing beside the cairn, a good distance off, and now the girl with black hair had joined them. They watched the three Vikings going in at the fifth door.

In Duncan's house were three half-grown children, two boys and a girl. 'Where is the purchaser of coats?' said Havard. 'Where is the ruination of poor weavers? Where is Duncan your father?'

'When the Viking ship came into the bay,' said a boy with fair hair, the oldest of the children, ' he took the mare from the stable and put our mother behind him on the mare's back and rode off south to visit his cousin Donald in Lairg.'

'What will you three do when we burn this house down?' said Arnor.

'We will stand outside,' said the boy, 'and we will be warm first and afterwards we will be cold.'

'And when we take away the coats for which Malcolm the weaver has not been paid?' said Arnor.

'Then we will be colder than ever,' said the boy.

'It is a clever child,' said Sven, 'that will doubtless utter much wisdom in the councils of Caithness in a few years' time. Such an orator should not go cold in his youth.'

They gave the children a silver Byzantine coin from their crusade the previous summer and left the house.

They found Kol where they had left him, at the wall, but he was dead. Someone had cut his throat with a corn-hook.

'Now we should destroy the valley,' said Havard.

'No,' said Arnor, 'for I'm heavy with the weaver's drink and it's getting dark and I don't want sickles in my beard. And besides all that the world is well rid of a fool.'

They walked down to the house where the sheep were tethered. Now eight dark figures, including Malcolm the weaver and Morag and the clever-tongued boy (Duncan's son), followed them all the way, keeping to the other side of the ridge. The men were armed with knives and sickles and hayforks. The moon was beginning to rise over the Caithness hills.

They killed the two sheep and carried them down the beach on their backs. The full moon was opening and shutting on the sea like the Chinese silk-and-ivory fan that Sven had brought home from Byzantium.

They had a good deal of trouble getting those awkward burdens of wool and mutton on board the *Eagle*.

'Where is Kol?' said Olaf the skipper.

'In a ditch with his throat cut,' said Sven. 'He was fortunate in that he died drunk.'

The Durness people stood silent on the beach, a score of them, and the old bereaved woman raised her hand against them in silent malediction.

The sail fluttered and the blades dipped and rose through lucent musical rings.

'The poem has two good lines out of seven,' said Olaf. 'I will work on it when I get home to Rousay.'

He steered the *Eagle* into the Pentland Firth.

TARTAN

Off Stroma he said, 'The tartan will go to Ingerd in Westray. Kol kept her a tattered trull all her days, but with this cloth she will be a stylish widow for a winter or two.'

A Carrier of Stones

1

DAG SIGURDSON who was a horse-dealer in Orphir said to Rolf the week after Rolf came back from his first viking cruise: 'Rolf, you are a young man and you have been a great deal in the news for what you did in England recently. Listen to me carefully. I have twelve horses in the hills of Harray and Orphir, some of them wild and scarcely to be trusted. You will hear sometimes a broken thunder on the far side of Revay. Also Thorkeld in Holm has two gray geldings that I lent him for the purpose of escorting the Earl and the Bishop through his estate in style last winter. Thorkeld has not sent those horses back to me. I do not trust Thorkeld. At the last horse-market in Kirkwall I gave Simon Flettir two crowns for his chestnut stallion called Thunder. Thunder has since earned him eleven fees but Thunder is not standing in my stable. Thunder is a beautiful horse and he belongs to me—see, here's the receipt—how low can men sink! This is what I want you to do, Rolf. I want you to collect all these horses that belong to me and I want you to drive them before midsummer to Greenay Hill in Birsay. If you do that, I will give you a gelding of your own choice out of my stables, and of course I will pay all your expenses.'

To this offer Rolf answered No.

2

A man called Hrug Paulson who farmed the Bu in Hoy wrote a letter to Rolf:

'Rolf, greeting.

'I am glad you have returned with honour and fame from the winter viking cruise in the south.

'Hold Ragnarson in Selwick is my neighbour, as you know. He has two ships and thirty cattle and a thousand sheep.

'His man Glum and my man Skop played draughts together some nights last winter in his bothy. One night there was a dispute over the board and Glum wounded Skop. He put his dagger between the fifth and sixth ribs of Skop on the right side, so that Skop lay sick in my house for a month afterwards till the wound healed.

'My grieve Arn went to Hold to get compensation for Skop's injury. They agreed on a fair sum. Hold said to Arn, 'I am going to send Glum away. He is lazy, besides being quarrelsome.'

'As Arn was riding back to the Bu, a man rose out of the ditch and hewed at him with an axe. Arn recognized the face of Glum between the flashings of the axe. Glum cut Arn deeply in the leg, then he turned and ran down the glen. Arn heard his scattered laughter among the rocks long after he disappeared.

'Arn will walk with a limp all the rest of his life. A tendon in his left leg was severed.

'I asked Hold for compensation for Arn's wound but Hold refused, saying that at the time the wound was given he had dismissed Glum from his service.

'So now there is bad blood between Hold and myself. This is a matter for deep regret. We were always good neighbours, Hold and I.

'Glum lives among the hills like a wolf now. Daily my shepherds find sheep with their throats cut. (As you know, I have five hundred sheep on The Ward and the Coolags and in the Trowieglen).

'It has come to this, even my shepherds are afraid to be alone on the hills.

'By night Glum comes down to the homestead and steals ale and meat and cheese from the cupboards.

'Last week a torch was put in the stable thatch and two horses burnt.

'He attacked the girl Ragna who was spreading out linen to dry on the grass beside the burn, and this morning we have sent Ragna home to her mother in Melsetter with sheeted eyes.

'Rolf, you are a famous man in the islands and on all the sea coasts as far as Scilly. Rid the islands of this beast Glum and it shall be to your profit and greater fame.'

Rolf sat down at once and wrote a refusal to Hrug Paulson.

3

The Laird's Hall in Sandwick, Orkney, a broad seaward facing room with tapestries and carved chairs and silver drinking cups on the high bench and a hound asleep at the fire.

Peter Solmundson the laird. Rolf.

PETER: Yes, Rolf. Well, Rolf. And did you have a good ride through the hills? Sit down. I'll tell you why I want to see you. Do you know how old I am? Eighty-seven. We'll eat in a minute. How many men did you lose in the Hebrides? Leif my nephew was wounded in the neck, I hear. And you were never so much as scratched. Rolf, they say you took that church in Armagh apart like a stone book. In my time they used to melt down the candle-sticks, I still have bits of holy silver about the house here. Yes, eighty-seven years old. The priest comes more often than he used to, most evenings, Father Orm. He says his Mass in my chapel out there. He reads to me, the life of some saint, Cormac or Brendan or somebody. I've spoken to the gravedigger, of course.

ROLF: It's best to be prepared.

PETER: Prepared, yes, I'm well prepared. Except for one thing. Rolf, I have four sons, four, but not one of them will have this Hall of Sandwick after me. Not one. Why not? Because—you must have heard, everybody knows, no point in hiding it—because they're all illegitimate. Do you know a man called Jouk who travels a stallion round the farms?

ROLF: Yes, I know Jouk.

PETER: He's one of them. Maril was his mother, a sweet little thing in her day, a milkmaid in the byres. That was in my father's time. And do you know Solm who's never out of the ale-house, a drunken thing?

ROLF: No.

PETER: He's another. I'm ashamed to own him but I must. And there's Grund who's a cook in the Earl's ship and Herman the sail-maker. Maril was not their mother.

ROLF: I know Grund.

PETER: They're all sons of mine. But here's the point, Rolf. I have three daughters by my dear wife Solveig who's been dead now fourteen years come Candlemas.

(*Cold crafty eyes, the skin about them warped like old leather purses. He dabs a diamond drop with his sleeve. True precious sorrow? Or counterfeit? It is hard to say, with such a man.*)

PETER: Three girls, Freya and Signy and Gretel. Do you know them?

ROLF: No.

PETER: Fine girls. But girls—what use are girls on a big estate like Sandwick? Eh? No use at all, Rolf. (Rolf, you're hungry.) There must be a man in authority, somebody to say to the ploughmen, 'Yoke today, get off your arses. . . .' After I'm dead, you understand. Someone to order the ships to Ulster, Jutland, Brittany, at the right

time of year with precisely the right cargo. . . . Rolf, the
place will go to pieces, I know that, to wrack and ruin,
this old famous wealthy estate of Sandwick. My great-
grandfather settled here first. I can trace my family back
five generations before that—merchants, farmers, vikings
—from Trondheim in Norway. My great-grandfather
ran his longship up the beach out there ninety-eight years
ago and he said, 'Put the plough on that hill, this is my
land. . . .' And he took the otter for his emblem because
the first living thing he saw when he landed was an otter
in the burn and he carved an otter over his door. I don't
want Roland the tinker eating off my silver plates. Rolf,
we'll eat in a minute, I can see you're hungry. Three
daughters. Of course I could easily get husbands for
them, but—(*He knocks on the floor with his stick.*) Freya's
been preparing a meal.

ROLF: I'm not hungry.

PETER: Freya now, she's a fine girl. Not a beauty
maybe. But marvellous hands on her. Do you see that
cloth behind the chair with the otter woven into it?
Freya wove that tapestry. The man who gets Freya will
have no complaints. No. Every comfort—grouse, lobster,
trout on the table, a fire in every room, a troop of servants
that don't answer back, order and decency everywhere,
the guests well entertained.

(*Freya comes in. Capable farm hands. Buttermilk,
honeycombs- the smell and the taste of her. Her womb is
awake. Her body is like a a banked-up forge waiting for the
thrust of love, the roaring bellows, masses of flame:
imagining, further on, cold shapes of plough and nail and
stirrup at the wall. Her body is like a swept barn in the days
before harvest with horses and cornstalks in the sun outside.
There will be another light, grass and buttercups, and another, children and birds in a snow-filled door taking from*)

her hands the broken bread. Her body is like a cupboard, empty and waiting.)

PETER: Freya. My dear girl. This is Rolf. The young man who did so well on the last viking cruise. (*Freya turns to Rolf, bows—is this her man?—sheds an uncertain smile, flushes.*) Well, Freya, and what have you got for us to eat, eh?

FREYA: Baked trout, father. New bread.

PETER: New bread, still smoking. Delicious. And what else?

FREYA: Lamb chops, father.

PETER: And what to drink?

FREYA: I broke a honeycomb in the March ale.

PETER: Did you? Good. Well now, Freya, will you take a bit of everything over to our guest here? Rolf is hungry, he's ridden over the hills specially to see us. Trout first.

ROLF: A cup of water, please, and a dry oatcake. That's all I want.

PETER: What, Rolf? Certainly. A dry—. . . Freya, that will be all.

(*Freya goes out uncaring. The world is full of gulls, ploughmen, children. Hunger and ripeness lie all about her. Her hour will come, the new seed quickening in the new furrow.*)

PETER: I'm not hungry myself. An old man of eighty-seven, what do you expect? . . . Rolf, is this true, that you're interested in music and poetry? I'm not very keen on that kind of thing myself. Always too busy, you know, with farm and ships. (*He knocks on the floor with his stick.*) I'd like very much—what I want is for you to meet my second girl, Signy. Signy is a talented girl. A lovely voice. That Iceland poet, whatsisname, was here last autumn, he stayed a week, and he said—

146

(*Signy comes in. Abundant bronze and ivory. A cold touch-me-not glance. She has heard of the battle by the morning sea, gules and glory, she wants no yokel heroes, Signy. Who is this clophopper who has sailed for a summer about the islands of the west and thinks himself song-worthy? She wants no hayseed heroes. Some day Siegfried's sail will break the horizon, virginal, and her virgin harp will go down to the rock to meet him.*)

PETER: Signy. Come here, Signy. Have you brought your harp? Signy, I want you to meet Rolf, a very famous young man indeed. An honour to have him in our house. (*Signy hardly so much as turns to Rolf*). I hope we'll be seeing a lot more of Rolf. Signy, Rolf wants very much to hear you singing.

(*Father Orm and one or two farm boys begin to chant the Litany of the Blessed Virgin Mary in the chapel.*)

FATHER ORM: *Mystical rose, pray for us.*
PETER: What's it to be? The Valkyries, eh? Music for heroes.
FATHER ORM: *Tower of David, pray for us.*
PETER: Wait a minute, I'll close this shutter. That's Father Orm at his wailing. We don't want any of that mournful stuff. (*He closes the shutter.*) Right, Signy.
SIGNY: (*singing, her voice a high cold powerful clang, bladed steel on granite.*)

> The warp is stretched
> For warriors' death.
> The weft in the loom
> Drips with blood.
> The battle darkens.
> Under our fingers
> The tapestry grows,
> Red as heart's blood,

147

Blue as corpses,
The web of battle.

PETER: Well, Rolf, what about that? There's more
verses to come. You know the way the Iceland poet
described Signy's voice—'bees in the ribs of a lion'.
Wasn't that a curious way to put it? I'll tell you what,
Rolf—nothing is worse than a clattering tongue in a
woman's skull. Nothing. And that Iceland poet, he said
this too—

ROLF: Can we have the shutter open?

PETER: The shutter? Signy, open the shutter.

ROLF: I'll open it myself.

(*Rolf opens the shutter and the litany is heard again.*)

FATHER ORM: *House of God, pray for us | Ark of the
covenant, pray for us.*

PETER: The next verse, Signy. Rolf, this is a marvellous verse, all sword-clash and thunder, listen.

ROLF: Poetry is the daughter of silence.

FATHER ORM: *Gate of heaven, pray for us | Morning
star, pray for us.*

PETER: Signy, you can go now. (*Signy goes out.*)
Silence, yes. Silence is a fine thing. Nothing wrong with
silence. I'll be getting plenty of silence soon. . . . Rolf,
there's just one thing I want to show you before you go.
This is really what I invited you here for. Just a minute,
I'll light a candle. It's after midnight. Is that priest still
at his prayers? No. Would you follow me, Rolf? It isn't
far.

(*Peter Solmundson leads Rolf through four rooms. In one
of them ploughman, shepherd, fisherman, sailor and
Roland the tinker are throwing dice under a lantern. They
pay no attention to Peter Solmundson and Rolf. Peter
dribbles his candle flame round them for a minute, hopeless-*

*ly, then he goes on, Rolf after him. In the fifth room a girl
is sleeping under a woven cover. The candle throws a
wavering pool of light about her head.)*

PETER: S-s-sh, Rolf. . . . We must be very quiet.
She's sleeping, the dear child. Rolf, this is my youngest
girl, my Gretel. Rolf, tell me this, what is the whitest
thing you've seen, eh?

ROLF: A swan rose out of the loch at Stenness as I
came past. It scattered water and light.

PETER: Tut, nothing.

*(The cover drawn back. Nakedness, nape to ankle a bright
bodyscape. The country of girlhood, alive in the slow
tautening and relaxation of ribs, sweet pulsations at
temple and wrist, a gentle flutter at the mouth, drift of a
single hair strand. An innocent kingdom, all apples and
shells, offered now so that vanity might grope contented
to the grave.)*

PETER: O gentle as a dove. Gretel is my dearest and
best. Rolf, is she not a beautiful girl?

ROLF: She is a very beautiful girl.

PETER: The man who marries this girl, he will own
all Sandwick, he and his sons after him. He will inherit
the gathered wealth of nine generations. I promise that.
Freya and Signy, they're nothing, a pastry-cook and a
screecher. Did ever you see such shoulder-blades?—like
shells. Beauty, innocence, wealth—here they are—what
more could the heart desire? Rolf, I have three ships
trading in Ireland. (*Gretel stirs in her sleep and turns over.*)
S-s-sh, we've been speaking too loudly. Listen to me,
Rolf. I'm a very old sick man. You can stay with Gretel
till morning. Yes. And with my blessing.

ROLF: (*at the door*) Speak to Roland the tinker.
Good night, Peter Solmundson.

(*Rolf goes out*).

PETER: Rolf! Please. . . . Rolf, come back! (*He sobs.
The carved otter over his door is a blank. Honour, art, and
grace have vanished into the enduring stone. There is no
viking axe to cut new heraldry in the lintel.*) Rolf!

(*Sound of hooves on the cobbles. The girl sleeps on. The
first wave of morning turns over a thousand glittering
shells out in the bay.*)

4

A Shetlander called Brun went to the horse market at
Firth that summer and challenged all-comers at wrestling.
Some of the strongest men in the islands wrestled against
Brun and they were all beaten. Lot the blacksmith who
could bend horse-shoes with his bare hands had his arm
broken so that he was never able to raise a hammer again.
The Shetlander took Magnus the helmsman of *The Maid
of Faroe* in a bear hug and cracked three of his ribs. That
night on the ship Magnus began to cough and spit out
blood. Before winter they dropped him off Cape Wrath
with stones at his feet.

On the second day of the horse-market no-one answered Brun the Shetlander's challenge when he stood on the
wall with his arms folded across his chest.

Brun the Shetlander laughed at the Orkneymen and
called them cowards.

A man in the crowd shouted, 'If Rolf was here, Brun,
you wouldn't have much to laugh about.'

Just then Rolf arrived at the market with a young horse
that he wanted to sell.

When the Orkneymen saw him they shouted 'Rolf!
Rolf!'

Rolf asked them what was the matter.

They told him how Brun the Shetlander had flattened all the strongest Orkneymen.

'He must be an able wrestler,' said Rolf.

Then they said that Brun was laughing at them all for cowards.

'He must be a very humorous man,' said Rolf.

Then they said that Rolf must go into the wrestling ring against the Shetlander, or the Orkneymen would be forever shamed.

Rolf said he was there to sell a horse and not to fight. 'I won't wrestle against Brun,' said Rolf.

The Orkneymen turned away from Rolf, so that he was left alone in the middle of the field with his horse.

Brun jumped down from the wall and stood before him. Rolf had never seen a more formidable man. His head was completely bald but he was very dark and hairy from nostril to navel. His arms hung low and they were thick as posts.

'Will you fight with me, Orkneyman?' said Brun.

'No,' said Rolf and held out his hand.

The Shetlander took Rolf's hand contemptuously and immediately began to scream. Dribblets of blood began to well from the burst points of his fingers. He went down howling on his knees in the mud. His hand and Rolf's were still welded together.

'I won't wrestle with you,' said Rolf, 'but I consider it an honour to shake hands with such a strong arrogant man as Brun.'

Then he took his horse's bridle and turned away to the dealer's stall.

Brun knelt weeping over the ruin of his hand for a long time. That same night he took boat for Shetland.

After that Rolf was the most famous man in all the north. Nobody disputed it.

5

Rolf was five years labouring with horses on a farm in Rinansay, but he did not get much peace because travellers and poets and men who wanted to make use of his strength were always knocking at his stable door. Also the vikings pestered him to go on another cruise.

He left Rinansay one winter and nobody knew where he went.

The stallion stood for a day at the headland, looking out to sea.

6

Sven of Westray who was an oarsman in Erling Ormson's ship the time that Earl Rognvald and Bishop William went on their pilgrimage of love and war and holiness through the Mediterranean to Jerusalem and Byzantium and Rome said when he got back to Orkney that he had seen Rolf in the Emperor's palace at Byzantium. Rolf lived in high honour there. He was a colonel in the Imperial Guard, the Varingars.

Sven said that Rolf was married to a Greek woman called Petra. Petra was a beautiful girl. But that did not prevent Rolf from seeking his carnal pleasures high and low in Asia and the Balkans. 'It is roses for him wherever he goes,' said Sven. 'The Patriarch refused to absolve him last Easter, a thing never heard of in the east before. . . .'

Rolf lived in a house of mosaic and tapestries, said Sven. He could speak the tongue of the Arabs. He had led a company of the Emperor's soldiery far into the desert and brought back much silver and Arab girls and mathematical equations. He had a Tartar horse that no man but himself could ride. He wore good stones on his hand, set in gold.

Rolf had not been very well pleased to see the Orkney-men.

'It's my opinion,' said Sven, 'that a man like Rolf was wise to leave a poor place like Orkney and look for fame and fortune in the great places of the world.'

But Sven was such a liar that not even his own mother could believe a word he said.

7

A traveller came to the gate of the monastery in Birsay in the Orkneys and asked to see the Abbot.

ABBOT: What are you wanting here?

TRAVELLER: Peace.

ABBOT: Work first, and peace after. Do you love God?

TRAVELLER: I don't know, Father.

ABBOT: Can you shift stones cheerfully? That amounts to the same thing.

TRAVELLER: I can shift stones.

ABBOT: There's a field out there full of stones. If there were no stones in it we could plough it out and grow corn.

TRAVELLER: I will shift the stones from the field.

ABBOT: There is a burn that flows down the hill. It comes down quickly to begin with, white and black over the stones, then it broadens into a quiet blue pool, then it ravels itself among a multitude of stones and so reaches the sea. If we got rid of the stones we could build a small mill above the sand and grind our own meal.

TRAVELLER: I will shift the stones from the burn.

ABBOT: Brother John who is an architect designed the mill three years ago. Having got rid of unnecessary stones both from the field and the burn, it will be necessary to carry useful stones from the shore for the building of the mill.

TRAVELLER: I will carry the stones.

ABBOT: But this labour though necessary is only of minor importance. The chapel must be kept clean for the offering of Mass and the daily singing of the Office. Our life is a life of prayer and praise and sacrifice.

TRAVELLER: I can use a brush and a cloth. Perhaps I will learn how to pray.

ABBOT: You will have to take off these clothes and wear a brown patched thing not much better than a scarecrow's coat. . . . What is your name, my son?

TRAVELLER: I wish to forget it.

ABBOT: You will be called Simon. The times you are doing nothing you can sit at the rock and fish, like your famous namesake. We need fish on Fridays especially.

TRAVELLER: I will fish whenever necessary.

So the traveller became a lay brother at the monastery in Birsay, and there he carried stones and set stones and learned at last, it may be, how to pray.

The Eye of the Hurricane

WHEN first I went to live in the ground floor flat of Captain Stevens's house on the hill behind Hamnavoe, three months ago, he would ask me every Friday afternoon to bring him from the licensed grocer's in the town a half-bottle of rum. He had a young woman, Miriam, who cleaned his room for him every morning and did his errands – a plain hard-working pleasant girl – but he never asked her to bring his week-end drink; possibly because Miriam's parents, and Miriam herself, were members of the Salvation Army, and might have conscientious objections.

It was no trouble for me to get his half-bottle of rum; Friday was the day I ordered my half-dozen cans of export beer, a modest quantity of drink that lasted me all week. I drank one can every evening between tea-time and supper-time.

The first Friday of February this year Captain Stevens came downstairs, knocked at my door and entered brusquely. 'I know it's only Friday morning, Barclay', he said, 'and I don't want to interrupt your work, but would it be too much to ask you to nip down to the town and get my rum as soon as it's convenient. I have a very heavy cold.'

'I'm sorry to hear that,' I said.

'A very heavy cold indeed,' he said. 'I spent too long the other day at the wreck, you know, the Danish fishing boat at the Kirk Rocks. Got my feet wet walking about her in the ebb.'

'There's where you caught your cold,' I said.

'Nowhere else,' said Captain Stevens. 'It's very good

of you to go.' He laid a five-pound note on the table.

It was in fact a great nuisance for me to oblige him just then. Every morning, between breakfast and lunch time, I work hard at my novel, and I let nothing distract me. In the afternoon I am at anybody's service; I keep that time for exercise; usually a walk along the Atlantic coast of the island, watching the movement of birds and water and clouds, or I might do some shopping in the town. Every evening I read or listen to the wireless, and drink my can of export. Very few friends call; I'm a stranger in the island; I don't find talk necessary; my writing comes before everything.

'I'm a bit busy, as you can see,' I said. The table was crowded with the paraphernalia of my trade—a writing pad crammed with the draft of a chapter, scored and interlined and transcribed in different colours of ink, a chaos unintelligible to anybody but myself; the partly-written fair copy on clean folded octavo sheets; blue and black and red biros; and the shrouded silent typewriter.

'I'm rather ill,' he insisted.

Well, I thought to myself, it will be an act of charity all the more meritorious because I don't want to do it. I am a Catholic and in the world as it is at present I find few opportunities for practising holy charity; the welfare state has abolished the poor and hidden the sick out of sight. I hope, in a vague kind of way, that writing is my work of charity, that perhaps my books bring solace and happiness to a few people that I have never seen or known. Here was one small extra opportunity to show that I was not altogether a timeserver in the kingdom of Christ.

'Thank you a lot,' said Captain Stevens as I put on my coat. 'Much obliged. Get me two full bottles of navy rum. The fiver will just cover it. I want this cold shifted by Monday—got a meeting of the Harbour Board that night.'

It struck me, as I walked down the steep road to the town, the captain doesn't look as if he had the cold, he isn't coughing or flushed or speaking thickly. There could of course be other more subtle symptoms.

I delivered the two bottles of rum in his upstairs room and finished copying the first third of Chapter Five before putting my Friday dinner to cook on the gas ring—smoked haddock simmered in milk and butter and thickened with corn flour and grated cheese.

Afterwards I walked along the coast as far as the Danish wreck, the *Dinesen*. She was poised high and dry among the rocks, masts and funnel and wheel-house intact, not a scratch on her. It seemed a pity, but the local men said she could never be refloated. She was lost as irretrievably as if the mid-ocean maelstrom had sucked her down. 'And,' said Dan Fraser the coastguard, leaning against the kirkyard wall smoking his pipe, 'there was no fog or gale to put her there. She went ashore last Wednesday, a bright mild afternoon if you remember. And there's her crew drinking and carrying on every night in the town, not caring one damn. If you ask me,' he said, 'they missed their drink and women and so they just deliberately piled her up where she is.'

That evening I was listening to an Ionescu play when I heard a couple of thumps on the ceiling over my head; it was Captain Stevens knocking. The wireless is on too loud, I thought, and lowered the volume. The knocking went on. Then I remembered he was unwell. When I entered his room he was in bed, and now he certainly had all the symptoms. His cheeks flared, he had watery eyes, the breath hurled in his chest, and he spoke thickly and inconsequentially.

'A terrible thing, Barclay,' he said. 'I dropped one of my bottles of rum, smashed it. Never do at all. I need the hot grog. If you open that drawer, Barclay, very kind of you, you'll see a wallet, there's a wad of notes in it, fivers. Take one of them. Got it? I don't mind your wireless being on at all, play it as loud as you like. Well, look, would you just nip down to Wilson's like a good chap and get me another bottle, no, better make it two while we're at it. Thanks a lot, you're very kind.'

Wilson was the licensed grocer.

As I walked down the road I couldn't help wondering about the broken bottle. While I was in Captain Stevens's room I had noticed the two rum bottles. One was three-quarters full and was standing on his bedside table (beside the framed photograph of a beautiful young woman) and the bottle on the mantlepiece was empty but unbroken.

As it happened, Wilson's was closed when I got there. I had to go along the street to the Hamnavoe Bar. The half-dozen fishermen from the *Dinesen* were inside, drinking lager beside the fire. They seemed to me to be inoffensive enough fellows.

*   *   *

Chapter Five of the novel went well next morning. I got up passing eight o'clock, had breakfast of tea and toast and a boiled egg, washed and shaved, said my prayers and began to write where I had left off yesterday. I stopped work in full flush at eleven o'clock to make some bovril. This flight that I had made from city to island was working out well. I had almost forgotten Sandra; all that remained of that summer affair was a criss-cross of scars in the spirit. Lovers with their new-sharpened senses set about chiselling a form of ideal desire, an Eros, that they can worship together till death; in the end, disillusioned, the finely-honed edges inflict ignorant vindictive surgery on one another. It was all over now, the long earnest discussions on sex and freedom and God, the Bartok and Monteverdi records, the Saturday afternoon strolls through the Botanic Gardens, the love-making in her flat after brandy and coffee (two fevered statues tumbled one on the other), the recriminations, confessions, resolutions. A phrase in Sandra's last letter sticks in my mind, 'We got out of our depths, you and I.' . . . It reminds me of a summer holiday by the sea when I was about seven. Another boy called Kim and myself played day after day on a rubber raft, navigating cautiously between the beach-balls and the white legs of old gentlemen paddling. One day we drifted further out. I looked down into undulating seaweed, a vast enchanted forest. Fish glinted from rock to rock like a silent torrent of knives. Kim and I laughed uncertainly to one another. Far out in the bay a steamer passed, and in her wake the raft bobbed and rocked and tumbled. Suddenly the bathing sheds and the donkeys seemed so far away that we could never return to that secure place—we were lost forever in this beautiful alien cruel element. We looked at each other with trembling lips, and Kim began to cry. An old fisherman rowed past from his lobster pots and towed us to the shore. For the rest of that holiday Kim and I avoided each other, we never exchanged so much as a single word. . . . That was the kind of way Sandra and I 'got out of our depths'.

I had come to live, then, among simple uncomplicated people. I worked to the easy regular rhythm of fishermen and crofters. My imagination nourished itself at primitive wholesome sources, the sea and the land. It seemed to me my writing had a depth and clarity I had never achieved before. (And of course I was working in the place where my novel was rooted. That was the reason, apart from Sandra, that I had come to live in the islands.)

There was a gentle tap at the door, and Miriam came in. 'I'm sorry to trouble you, Mr Barclay,' she said, 'but it's the captain."

'Is his cold worse?' I said.

She looked with fleeting horror at the crucifix on my wall and the porcelain Virgin-and-child on the dresser. Then she said, 'He hasn't got a cold, and I'm more than surprised at you, Mr Barclay, bringing drink to an old man who was at death's door twice last year with rum.'

'I'm sorry,' I said. 'I didn't know.'

'You know now,' she said. 'Never take a drop of drink to him, especially when he's on one of his bouts. He nearly died twice last year. He's getting old, he can't stand it so much now as he used to. You see, he's been having bouts ever since I can mind, three or four times a year. He spends a fortune. And he won't eat a bite so long as there's drink in his room. I tell you what it is, he only began to drink after Mrs Stevens died ten years ago. She was a beautiful person. They were only married a year. Then God took her.'

'I'm sorry,' I said.

'Please,' Miriam said, 'you must help me. The best thing you can do is say No when he asks you to get him more rum from the town. Just say No. He won't be pleased at the time, but after it's over he'll thank you. Promise.'

'All right,' I said. 'I promise.'

'Thank you,' said Miriam. 'Thank you very much indeed.'

'How long do they last, his bouts?' I said.

'About a week,' said Miriam.

I did no more work on Chapter Five that morning. I could hear upstairs the broken music of their dialogue—

though no distinct words came through the ceiling – the curt voice of Captain Stevens and the gentle pleadings of the girl; then a loaded silence.

I put away my writing things.

I spent the afternoon at the shops, buying fish and meat and groceries for the weekend, and arranging for a taxi to take me the fifteen miles to Mass in Kirkwall next morning.

Now that Miriam had prepared me for some days of tension in the house, I wasn't surprised when a summons came early in the evening, three loud irregular thumps on the ceiling.

He was sitting beside the fire in an old dressing-gown. He hadn't washed his face, an unusual thing, for he was a neat spruce little man. There was no sight of bottles or glasses anywhere, but I breathed thick sweet treacly air. The rum ritual was being observed in secrecy.

'Come in, Barclay,' he said. 'Pleased to see you. Sit down over there.'

'How's the cold?' I said.

'So-so,' he said. 'We'll talk about that in a minute. The writing going along fine?'

'Moderately,' I said.

'That's no life for a man, writing,' said the captain. 'Do some real work, get a croft or a fishing boat, that's the thing. You should have a woman. I wish I was young, I wish I had my time over again. I'd show them. I would do a lot of things different.'

'I think you've made a real success of your life,' I said. 'Commodore of the shipping line. The O.B.E. County councillor. Chairman of the Harbour Board.'

'Salt and ashes,' he said. 'Now, Barclay, about this cold of mine.'

'Miriam says you haven't got a cold at all,' I said.

'The little bitch,' he said. 'Did she go into your room? She had no right to be disturbing you. I'll speak to her about that. I expect she told you also that I have drinking bouts.'

'She did,' I said.

'Well,' he said, 'everybody knows. Can't do a thing about it, Barclay. It's a natural thing, like a storm, you just have to let it blow itself out, keep the ship headed into it. Do you understand that, Barclay?'

'I know nothing about it,' I said.

'I thought writers are supposed to understand things,' he said, 'the quirks of human nature. That's what they're for. Don't take hard what I say, Barclay. I like you. I'm very glad you're living in this house. I'm just explaining the situation to you, setting the course through the storm, so that you can take your turn at navigating if the need arises. The best way you can help the voyage, Barclay, is just do what I say. I'm the skipper of this ship. And the first thing I want you to do is open that drawer and you'll see a wallet.'

'No,' I said, and got to my feet.

'There should be four five-pound notes in it. Take one of them out.'

'No,' I said.

'Two bottles of navy rum from Wilson's, as quick as you can.'

Charity is no hard-minted currency to be distributed according to whim, a shilling here and a sovereign there – it is the oil and wine that drop uncertainly through the fingers upon the wounds of the world, wherever the roads of pity and suffering cross. It might help this old man, as he said, if I stood close beside him on the bridge till this particular hurricane blew itself out. But I trusted the older wisdom of women. I had made a promise to Miriam.

'No,' I said.

'Very well, Mr Barclay,' he said after a pause. 'Let me see. At the moment you are paying me a rent of two pounds a week, I think. As from Monday next you will pay me four pounds a week. In fact, I think you should make arrangements to leave this house before the end of the month. I find you an unsatisfactory tenant. Now get out.'

All night, till I fell into a drowse around three o'clock in the morning, I heard him pacing back and fore, back and fore in his room, an ancient mariner in a ship of dark enchantment.

*　　*　　*

Chapter Five got wedged in some deep rut of my mind. I sat most of a morning with my black biro poised over the writing pad. The phrases and sentences that presented themselves were dull, flaccid, affected. I looked blankly at the crucifix on the wall, but the Word that spanned all history with meaning was only a tortured image. The words I offered to the Word were added insults, a few more random thorns for the crown. I scored out everything I had written since breakfast time.

It flatters us writers to think of ourselves as explorers, probing into seas that have never been mapped, or charted with only a few broken lines. But the spacious days of 'Here be Whales', cherubs puffing gales from the four quarters, mid-ocean mermaids, are gone for ever. There is nothing new to find; every headland has been rounded, every smallest ocean current observed, the deepest seas plumbed. Chaucer, Cervantes, Tolstoy, Proust charted human nature so well that really little is left for a novelist like myself to do. For the most part we voyage along old trade routes, in rusty bottoms; and though we carry cargoes of small interest to anyone—

coal or wheat—we should be glad that hungry cupboards here and there are stored with bread and there are fires burning in cold snow villages of the north.

Miriam came in without knocking. 'The captain's had a terrible night, the poor man,' she said. 'There's six broken cups in the sideboard. The rug's saturated. He was trying to make himself a pot of tea, and his hands all spasms. He never so much as closed an eye.' She had her coat on to go home for, as I said, she only works in the house mornings.

'He wanted me to get him more rum,' I said, 'two bottles, but I wouldn't do it.'

'You were right,' said Miriam.

'He's going to put me out on the road,' I said.

'Don't worry about that,' said Miriam. 'That was the devil talking, not the poor captain at all. Once he's better he won't know a thing he's said this past day or two.'

'I'm glad,' I said, 'because I like it here.'

'It must be lonely for you,' said Miriam. 'You should come to our Joy Hour some Thursday evening. There's choruses and readings from the Good Book, and O, everybody's so happy!' Her eyes drifted uneasily over the crucifix and the Virgin.

I said nothing.

'I'm pleased with you,' said Miriam, 'for saying No to him. He'll suffer, but his bout'll be over all the sooner. Tomorrow, or the day after, he'll be his old self again.'

There came a violent double thump on the ceiling. 'Get off, you bitch!' roared Captain Stevens. 'What are you talking to that pansy for? This is my house. Away home with you!'

Miriam lowered her voice. 'Be firm for one day more,' she whispered. 'He'll try to wheedle you in the afternoon for sure. I know him. Just keep saying No.'

'I will,' I said.

'If only Robert Jansen and Stony Hackland keep away,' whispered Miriam. 'You mustn't let them in. If they come to the door just send them packing. Be very firm.'

'Who are they?' I said.

'Seamen who used to sail in his ships,' she whispered. 'They carry the drink in to him whenever he has a bout.'

'They won't get in,' I said.

When she smiled her plain little face shone for a moment like one of Botticelli's angels.

If she had been born in a Breton village, I thought, she would be a devout Catholic girl, and rosary and image and candle – that she shied away from with such horror – would be the gateway to her dearest treasures and delights. As it was, she merely touched the hem of Christ's garment in passing.

The weather continued mild. But the *Dinesen* showed a deterioration when I walked beyond the Kirkyard on Monday afternoon. The sea lay high and bright about the wreck – one thought of water on such a day as the gentlest of the elements – yet sometime during the weekend it had lifted the boat and set her down at a slightly different angle, against a rock, so that she looked now for the first time like some utterly helpless thing, and the mast sagged from the deck like a broken limb.

I was cooking my bacon-and-eggs on the gas ring at five o'clock, glancing ocasionally through the window over the road and the town and harbour. A very old man was struggling up the road, carrying a loaded hold-all, and stopping every now and again to get his breath. It was a painful climb for such a frail creature. Then he turned in at our gate, and I saw that it was Captain Stevens. The door opened; I heard his quick harsh breathing in the lobby; he climbed the stair to his room. He was home, under his own steam, with another cargo of rum.

I settled down for an evening of reading, Alain-Fournier's *Le Grand Meaulnes*, an exquisite rural idyll, as far removed as could be from salt and rum; but I wasn't surprised when, soon after eight o'clock in the evening, the interruption came. 'Barclay!' roared Captain Stevens from the stair-head, 'I want to see you, double quick, no hunkersliding, at once!'

I went upstairs.

He was standing at the table, supporting himself with his fists. There was a half-empty bottle on the table and a full bottle on top of his television set and three with various quantities of rum in them ranged along the mantleshelf. He was very drunk and angry. 'Barclay,' he said, 'you understand this is a matter for the police. As soon as we dock I will report you.'

'What for?' I said.

'Don't come the holy simpleton with me,' said Captain Stevens. 'You and your fancy-women! Do you think I'm going about this ship deaf, blind, and stupid! Is that what you think? Barclay, I know this for a fact, last night you had Merran Muir and Thora Romanski and Celia Thomson in your cabin. Did you or did you not? A straight answer now.'

'I did not,' I said.

'You're a liar, Barclay. I won't have this ship turned into a whore-house. I intend to report you to the police. Meantime I confine you to your cabin.'

I turned to go. My hand was on the door-knob when he spoke again. 'I have reason to believe,' he said in a low even voice, 'that you're trying to seduce little Miriam. You will not speak to her in future. You will not so much as look at her. For if you do, by God, old

man as I am, I'll thrash you within an inch of your life.
Now get out.'

The bitter sea had invaded the wheatfields and lakes
of *Le Grand Meaulnes*; the delicate masque was drenched,
dragged under, drowned. I tried to read a few more
pages, but it was no good. I went to bed and lay sleepless
for hours. Near midnight he shouted from the stair-head,
'I once had a black woman.'

Later there were some bursts of laughter from his
room, and once I thought he was crying, and once a cup
went over on the floor with a small crash.

Then all sounds guttered into silence.

*   *   *

My novel is about the holy voyage of Rognvald
Kolson, Earl of Orkney, who sailed from Norway to
Palestine (Guthaland, 'God's country' the Norsemen
called it) in 1150-51. With Earl Rognvald in fifteen ships
sailed the Bishop of Orkney, a group of brilliant Icelandic
poets, and the greatest captains of the north–Thorbjorn
Black, John Peterson, Erling Ormson, Solmund Fish-
hook, Eindred Young. The voyage was rooted in pure
intention; it was to be a pilgrimage, a penance, a God-
faring, to redeem the time, to delete from history the
Viking hawkfall. 'We must wash a great quantity of
crusted blood from our hands,' said Earl Rognvald.
Christianity had been crudely grafted on to Scandinavia
a century and a half earlier. 'But you do not make saints
out of savages overnight,' said Bishop William of Orkney. 'The leaven needs time to work.' The pilgrims who
took the dove's path to Jerusalem were in fact not radi-
cally different from their fathers who had torn harp and
tapestry and fleur-de-lys all over the west less than a
century before. Events took place during this holy voyage
–the landfall and banqueting in Narbonne, the siege of

the Spanish castle, the attack on the Saracen ship—which Earl Rognvald chose to regard as flowers of Christian chivalry; but the roots went deep into the dark history that was to be sanctified. 'See how well they change their praying hands back into claws,' said the Bishop. 'We had better say a Mass on the deck *every* morning.'

I had made a satisfactory start with the ordering of the great ships in Norway, the craft of the shipwright, the recruitment of seamen, the Orkney wintering, a great storm in the Bay of Biscay and the passage through the Strait of Gibraltar, in the first four chapters. This was straightforward stuff, boisterous, epic, gay. The fifth chapter required altogether different treatment. At the seaport of Narbonne in France, Earl Rognvald, paying a courtesy call, met the countess of the place, a young widow called Ermengarde. That evening, among the wine cups and the lutes, they looked at each other, their eyes faltered, their lips fell silent. There is a small delicious silence in the saga also; but after a winter in Narbonne the Iceland skalds, and Earl Rognvald himself, made rapturous lyrics about their French hostess as the sails flew eastward. The common seamen had got their satisfaction and their poxes in the stews of Narbonne. In the palace had been enacted a romance of the rose, passionate and chaste. In this Chapter Five I had some-how to communicate to the twentieth-century common reader, accustomed to the last hectic boring obscenities of romantic love, its sacred ceremonial root. Eight hundred years ago in southern Europe men turned from phallus-and-rut, child getting, family alliances, marriage settlements. The scales dropped from their eyes. The love lyric was born between fountain and first nightin-gales. Where did it come from, this dawning wonder at the mystery of Woman? Devotion to the Virgin, 'mystical rose', was one source. Also a new profane skill intrigued men at this time: the cultivation of gardens. Lovers became initiates of multifoliate mysteries, penetrating stage by stage beyond the stone masks of sickness, age, impotence, that hold the garden bewintered. Enchanted with promise of April, they seek the rosebush; and pluck often, not heart's-desire, but a cluster of wounds.

'Come and help me at once, please,' cried Miriam from the door. Her face was white and blank as a mushroom. I followed her up the stair. Captain Stevens was lying on his back on the floor, his feet under the table and his head in the fireplace. His eyes were open and he seemed to be conscious of what was happening, but he was absolutely paralytic. Miriam took his feet and I took his shoulders and we heaved him into bed, boots and all. Miriam covered him with a blanket and a coat. 'Much obliged,' he muttered. 'Thank you. A rough night, shipmates.'

There were empty rum bottles everywhere; one in the fireplace, one on the mantleshelf, one on the table beside the photograph of Mrs Stevens. There was a full bottle on the sideboard and another two-thirds empty on the small television table – Miriam emptied them both down the sink. 'Well,' she said, 'he won't get to any licensed grocer today, that's one thing sure. He's too helpless.'

'Miriam,' came the mumble from the bed, 'don't leave me.'

'I've a good mind to leave you for good,' she said sharply, 'but I won't, because then there'd be only the devil and yourself.'

'How's the old ship standing up, eh, to this battering?'

'Go to sleep,' said Miriam. 'Get that nonsense about ships out of your head. You're in a house on dry land and you're half dead with rum, and you've got friends trying to help you.'

At the foot of the stairs I said to Miriam, 'He's going to put the law on me. He says I'm taking prostitutes into the house. He says I have bad intentions towards you.'

'Pray for him,' she said gently, and went back upstairs.

I arranged the rough draft of Chapter Five on the table and took up my biro. Nothing happened. In the rose garden of Narbonne a small white hand lay in a hand rough as barnacles. A communication, something between lust and sanctity, trembled in that green place, an unspoken dialogue. Somewhere, hidden in leaves, a bird began to sing. . . .

The weather continued mild. The sea rose gently round the *Dinesen* and broke the wreck into trembling reflections. But, silently and inexorably, it was tearing the boat apart. And today the local men were taking a hand in the game. They were carrying pots, lamps, spars, drums of oil out of the boat when I rounded the corner of the kirkyard. 'There'll be trouble about this,' Dan Fraser assured me, squirting brown tobacco juice at the kirkyard wall. 'Nobody gave them permission to do that. I warned them. Next thing you see, the police'll be here.'

I wandered into the graveyard. This was the first tombstone I stopped to read:

ELIZABETH STEVENS
1930 - 1956
MICHAEL STEVENS
born and died
June 1956

When I got back to the house passing three o'clock Miriam was buttoning up her coat in the lobby.

'I'm very glad you're back,' she said. 'I cleaned him up

as best I could. I must go now. . . .' She opened the front door. 'Please stay in the house. He's asleep. He won't be able to take one step for drink this day, thank God. I'm feared all the same the horrors come on him, like they did that time last summer when he saw the Irishmen and the clocks everywhere.'

'I wouldn't know what to do,' I said.

'Just send for me,' she said. And then she did a most sweet and unexpected and trustful thing—she stood on tiptoe in the open door and leaned quickly forward and put her mouth to my mouth—a kiss small and chaste as a snowflake. She was gone before I could say a word.

The house was silent as prayer all the rest of the afternoon. I was about to light my paraffin lamp (there is an electric bulb in the ceiling but I much prefer the soft diffused radiance of oil) when I thought I heard the captain stirring above. I tiptoed upstairs and lifted the flap of his letter-box and listened. Everything was quiet.

I felt very tired, not having slept properly for nights. I sat down in the stair, midway between the captain's room and my own, and put my head in my hands. And all at once, quite involuntarily, a scheme of seduction arranged itself in my mind, and unfolded sombrely and inevitably. It concerned Miriam and myself. We moved together from station to station of lust—initial coldness, then conspiracy, shared stratagems, gratitude, a single kiss in a doorway, an offered flower, the sacrifice of a maidenhead. I saw with piercing clarity Miriam lying, white and broken and satiated, in the large double bed in my room, under the paraffin lamp, the ship's wheel, the crucifix.

So in the dark stairway of Captain Stevens's house I arranged the absurd antique ballet. The white hart stirred behind the trees; the quiver was loaded; the dogs of lust raised near and far their broken music. . . .

The front door slammed open violently, feet thumped and voices called in the lobby downstairs. 'Be quiet there!' I whispered sharply over the bannister. I could see nothing. I came down and stood on the first step. Two huge men loomed in front of me. One of them had a canvas ships-bag on his back and it clanked with loaded glass. The other man—I recognized him, he was the simple-minded sailor Robert Jansen who wandered the streets every Saturday night looking for his drowned friend Walls—had two unmistakable bottle shapes under his reefer jacket. 'Hello, Mr Barclay,' he said gently. 'This is my friend Stony Hackland. We're just going up to see the skipper.'

'You can't see him,' I said. 'It's impossible. Captain Stevens is very ill.' I put my foot against the bannister so that they couldn't get past.

'Off the gangplank, shipmate,' said Stony Hackland. His enormous hand closed on the lapels of my jacket. He swung me about and pressed me as flat as a gate against the wall. The two seamen went on upstairs past me.

'You see, Mr Barclay,' said Robert Jansen, 'the captain said Stony and me were to come tonight for sure.'

Stony Hackland flung open the door of Captain Stevens's room. 'It's us, skipper, Hackland and Jansen reporting.' A shape stirred and queried in the interior darkness. Robert Jansen quietly shut the door. I was excluded.

Back in my own room I opened a can of export and sipped the cold beer and wondered what to do. I would have gone for Miriam at once, but mortification over the masque of rape I had entangled her in, held me back. Besides, what could a girl like her do against two hulking brutes like Hackland and Jansen? The old man is saturated as a sponge, I thought, he can't hold any more rum. Maybe the company of seamen is just what he needs at this moment? Then bottles began to clank in the room above. I thought of the doctor and the police.

There was suddenly such a terrific crash above that the mugs shivered and clinked in my cupboard. I leapt up the stairs and opened the door. The table had gone over, the floor was a chaos of glass, seeping rum, cups, tulip bulbs, earth, pieces of porcelain and crystal.

Captain Stevens was standing between bed and rocking chair in his dressing gown. Stony Hackland and Robert Jansen stood in front of him, their caps in their hands. Captain Stevens eyed me coldly. He gestured and pointed. I went over and stood beside the sailors.

'Gentlemen,' he said in a quiet grave voice, 'I want you to know exactly what the position is. You are naturally wondering about Captain Falquist, you haven't seen him on the bridge all day. I must tell you that Captain Falquist died last night in his cabin, suddenly. He was a very good man, a very pleasant man. We have lost a friend. I am now in command of this ship, at least until such time as we arrive back in port. You will take your orders from me without question.

'This has been an unlucky voyage, I don't need to impress that on you. Trouble right from the start with the seamen, if you can call them seamen, most of them are better acquainted with the inside of a prison cell. I don't intend to be soft with them like Captain Falquist, God rest him. The hurricane *seems* to be over. But don't delude yourselves, gentlemen. We are only passing through the quiet centre of it. We must prepare ourselves for more tempest, more trouble of all kinds, I'm afraid. The cargo is loose in the hold for one thing. It constitutes a danger to the ship and the lives of the crew. Do I make myself clear?'

'Yes sir,' said Stony Hackland and Robert Jansen together.

Captain Stevens turned to the mantleshelf and with a steady hand poured out three glasses of rum and handed one to Jansen and one to Hackland and one to me. 'I'm not a drinking man myself,' he said, 'never have been. So I won't join you. But for the remainder of this unfortunate trip I wish you all luck and courage.'

'Cheers, captain,' said Stony Hackland.

'Courage,' said Captain Stevens, 'by God we need courage more than we need money or clothes or sleep. We need it all the time. Cradle and coffin, they're both shaped like ships—you'll have noticed that—and it's a desperate and a dangerous voyage we all have to make, from birth into death and beyond it. Even the pen-pusher who sits at a desk all day with papers and ink. We all need courage.'

He paused for a minute, then said quietly, 'There is only one thing more important than courage—love.' He suddenly glared at Stony Hackland. 'Take that smirk off your face, Hackland,' he shouted.

'Sorry, sir,' said Stony Hackland.

'The love of women,' said Captain Stevens, 'a very precious jewel. I have known men lucky enough to possess it. They had a completeness in their lives, these lovers, everything they did seemed to be well done, faithfully done, even when it wasn't. I think of them now and I envy them bitterly, because, personally speaking, this gift of love has passed me by. I'm an old man now, I can never know what it is. (Spasms of lust, I've had them all right, but that's quite another thing.) I'm not complaining, mind you. I suppose I must thank God for the one crude gift he's given me, courage. I think I may need it before this trip's over.'

'Courage,' muttered Robert Jansen, and raised his glass. We all drank, except the captain.

'At least you can depend on courage,' said Captain

Stevens. 'There's no substitute for courage when the time comes. But love—what counterfeits, what frauds and imitations it's given rise to! Poor Falquist—the fly-by-night he tied himself to, by God, though she was five hundred miles away at the time, she and no other held the gun to his head and pulled the trigger. And I've known worse than her, many, much worse.' He turned to me. 'You,' he said, 'what's your name again, I forget?'

'Barclay, sir,' I said.

'Are you married, Barclay?' he said.

'No, sir.' I said.

'Get yourself a good wife, Barclay,' he said. 'We're going through the shining eye of the hurricane. It'll only last two hours, three at the most, don't delude yourselves. . . . I want you, Barclay, to go down and have a look at the cargo and come back here and report. It'll soon start blowing again and then you won't be able to go.'

He swayed and fell against the television set as if he had been axed at the knees. The box shuddered and slid to the floor and seemed to explode; valves and coils were flung all over the room. My hand was scratched by a bit of flying glass.

Stony Hackland bent over Captain Stevens and raised him by the shoulders. 'Wind's getting up,' he said.

I went straight from the house into the cold starlight and down to the small house on the pier where Miriam lived with her parents.

All the way back she only spoke once. 'You promised to look after him,' she said.

When Miriam and I arrived Robert Jansen and Stony Hackland had got the old man back into his bed, but only, it seemed, after a struggle. The room was a worse shambles than ever; the curtain was half ripped from the pelmet and a black star had exploded across the mirror; the only thing left standing was the photograph of

Elizabeth Stevens on the bedside table. Captain Stevens didn't seem to recognize Miriam at first. She bent over him and put his lead-blue hands back under the blanket. 'No women on this ship,' he mumbled. 'Be put ashore first port.'

'Yes,' said Miriam,' and it won't be long till we're there. The storm's blowing done.'

Stony Hackland and Robert Jansen sat in the fireplace drinking the last of the rum out of cups. 'He's the decentest skipper ever I sailed with,' said Stony Hackland. 'Strict, but very fair in his dealings.'

'A straight shooter,' said Robert Jansen.

Miriam's lips moved soundlessly over the stiffening face on the pillow. He opened his eyes once and looked at her. 'Elizabeth,' he said.

Then blindness, silence, cold.

Miriam turned towards the two drunk men in the fireplace. 'You'll be pleased to know,' she said, 'that you've killed Captain Stevens.'

Robert Jansen began to cry.

To me she said coldly, 'Get Dr Wilson.'

*　　*　　*

On the three mornings before the funeral I did no work on Chapter Five. I made myself a bite to eat, took an abrupt walk among the fields before returning to the shrouded house, read beside the fire till it was dark. The night before the funeral I read the penitential psalms and the prayers for the dead over and over again till their austerities were only a confusion of dark syllables and I dropped off to sleep in the arm-chair. It was no empty piety; I was concerned that the soul of that brave heart-broken man should have secure anchorage at last, somewhere.

Miriam came to the house every morning as usual.

She was a whole day clearing up the debris of the final rum tempest, a formidable task, and she had to be there to receive visitors—the provost, the minister, county councillors, members of the Harbour Board, the captain's relatives (three old people who arrived from the island of Quoylay the night before the funeral, and had to be accommodated) and some of those stray flower-bearers who are always attracted by the paraphernalia of death. The undertaker came twice or thrice a day.

Miriam paid no attention to me. She left me among my sacred and profane images. I knew she considered that I had betrayed her; and so I had, but after another fashion, with my lascivious imagination.

It was a fine afternoon when they buried Captain Stevens beside his wife and son. A cluster of mourners stood among the tombstones with bared heads. The huge back of Robert Jansen shook with grief. The minister prayed. Eight seamen lowered the coffin into the grave. I stood beside the broken wall of the pre-Reformation church. *Requiem aeternam dona ei, Domine.*

The minister closed his book and the knot of mourners broke apart. The gravedigger got busy with his shovel. Another cell in this honeycomb of death was being sealed.

Beyond the churchyard wall, on its reef, the *Dinesen* had completely disintegrated. Nothing remained but her hull, a hollow cave for the sea, and the next storm would strew the beach with boards and leave only a skeleton among the rocks. Dan Fraser still stood on guard over her, smoking his pipe.

The kirkyard of Hamnavoe is two miles from the town, and so the mourners are transported there and back by bus. I happened to find myself beside Stony Hackland in the front seat.

'Tell me,' I said, 'about Captain Falquist.'

He wrinkled his brows at me. 'That was the *Orlando*,' he said. 'Fancy you knowing about that.' . . . It was obvious that Stony remembered nothing about the bacchanal on the night of Captain Stevens's death.

'Is it true,' I said, 'that Captain Falquist committed suicide?'

'Shot himself,' said Stony. 'Officially it was accidental death. We buried him at sea, off Bermuda. "Misadventure while cleaning his gun", Captain Stevens reported when we got back, and that's what appeared in the newspaper reports and, I suppose, on his death certificate. We all knew he shot himself, all the same. He was too kind a man for skipper of a rough ship like the *Orlando*. It was a very unlucky trip. The crew, they were bad for a start, a lot of them newly out of Walton jail in Liverpool. Captain Stevens was first officer that trip. He knew how to handle them. If it hadn't been for him there'd have been murder and mutiny, sure as hell, in the first few days. As it was, they nearly killed the cook. Two days out of Boston we ran into this hurricane. Worst I ever seen. I swear I said my prayers six times a day, a thing I never did before or since. There was old Falquist up on the bridge with his long kind sad face, and Mr Stevens the first officer beside him with a face like a hunk of granite. And that night the cargo shifted, American clocks and other machinery, very delicate, very valuable— a hundred enormous containers lumbering about in the hold like elephants. And there was them bloody jailbirds down below, scared as rats, and all the more vicious because they were frightened. It wasn't a piece of cake for any skipper.

'Some kind of a personal message came through early next morning for Captain Falquist—God knows what it was—they say he was married to one of *them* kind of women, you know, that keep their treasure between their thighs and trade in any market, very pretty but treacherous as hell—God knows—be that as it may, old Falquist takes the sheet of paper from the radio officer and reads it and walks straight to his cabin and a minute after that there was this sound of one shot. And all this time, remember, the ship's wallowing about in great bloody chasms of sea, and her innards all loose. . . . We never knew about it till the hurricane was over. All we knew was, that kind good face was missing from the bridge and in its place that chunk of granite. It scared us and it put heart in us.

'That same summer Captain Stevens met his wife, a Birsay woman, Elizabeth Halcrow, very young and pretty, and in no time at all he was married to her.

'Next voyage he was given his own ship. Not before time either—the directors didn't like him because he spoke hard and direct, he never was one of your arse-lickers—that delayed his promotion. All the same, he was commodore of the line before he retired.'

The bus halted at the Pier-head. Stony Hackland got off with the other seamen and they all went into the Hamnavoe Bar.

Alone in the empty house that night, I turned the knob of my radio through sudden frenzies of jazz, staccato morse, a welter of foreign voices, till it came to rest in a temple of solemn sound.

It was the last movement of a quartet—possibly Beethoven; I know little about music.

The viola, a sybil, surged with deep subtle questionings, and the violins, innocent creatures of April, were pierced with the pain and loveliness of desire, and the cello said over and over again, *Lamb of God, Have mercy on us, Grant us peace.*

The pang of the violins was taken by the viola and turned into wise sad proverbs: *Beauty passes, Joy is a dream, Love uncertain.* The cello reassured, *Have no fear, Apple and dove, Thy Kingdom come.*

The violins trysted and parted and came together again, young tormented lovers. *No,* said the viola, *Misery is everywhere, Love is a shadow, Make your hearts marble.* And the cello seemed to contradict its former piety with a long sorrowful utterance, *Death is sure, Dust unto dust, All is vanity.*

There was a brief silence.

Then all the instruments consented in a final dance, Love and Wisdom and Holiness crowned one another with garlands. The violins fled away. The viola covered their going with wise greenery. The cello, alone on the steps of the temple, brimmed with benediction: *God is good, All is well, Rest in peace.*

*　　*　　*

Three weeks have passed since the death of Captain Stevens.

I have completed Chapter Six of *The Holy Voyage* (The Siege of the Spanish Castle) and Chapter Seven (The Attack on the Saracen Ship) writing a thousand fluent words every morning between breakfast and lunch. Everything has gone well. I have taken deep pleasure in the work; in the cold hawkflight of the Viking pilgrims I have got release from the sorrow and confusion that engulfed this house so suddenly.

Chapter Five remains unfinished. I shall return to it later, when a great deal that is confused and uncertain now clarifies in my mind. Love is too deep a subject for prose—only music and poetry can build bridges between the rage of the seed in the furrow, the coupling of beasts, the passion of man and woman, the saint's prayer. Seed and beast and saint are touched with simple fire. The loves of Thorkeld Stevens and Elizabeth, of Earl Rognvald and the Lady Emengarde, of Robert Jansen and Walls, of Captain Falquist and his fly-by-night, of myself and Sandra, seem to be nothing but chaos, loss, heartbreak. I know, though I cannot celebrate it, that all these loves are caught up in their true order, and simplified, and reconciled, in the wheel of being whose centre is Incarnation; they move about it forever like the quiet stars.

I do not know how much longer I can stay here. I met the lawyer in the street one day last week. He told me that the house is to be advertised for sale as soon as possible.

I must begin to look for another place.

On Saturday evening, after a week of hard pleasurable work, I walked down to the town. The Hamnavoe Bar was crowded with crofters and fishermen and sailors. The crew of the *Dinesen* were there; they were all happy because now there was no chance at all that their boat could be refloated, and the order for their recall had come. They were due to fly home from Kirkwall on Monday morning. Once Robert Jansen came in looking for his drowned friend Walls and went out again. A young Dane with a curled golden beard bought drinks for everyone in the bar. Stony Hackland was very drunk. He had his arms round the shoulders of two Danes and as they swayed together above the fire he was telling them that Scandinavians were the best seamen in the world, always had been since the first ships were built. 'The boat you wrecked on the Kirk Rocks,' said Stony, 'just bloody bad luck, shipmates, could happen to anybody, not to worry, seaman myself.' The young bearded skipper ordered another double whisky for Stony Hackland.

I left the pub and walked along the dark street. Round the fountain at the pier-head the twelve Salvationists stood in a ring, and a few drunks lay against the Custom House wall listening to the holy ragtime.

'*Will your anchor hold in the storms of life?*' the songsters chanted. Miriam rattled her tambourine among the shining trumpets. The big drum thudded at her side. Her face was radiant under the street lamps.